F & B English

一本搞定內外場

王郁琪 ◎著

餐飲英語

全面提升「即答力」，打造「薪動力」

詳盡主題 　12個單元，涵蓋48種餐飲職場工作情境

情境對話 　真實的職場情境會話，超過365組的應對話術，從工作中學英文，從英文學習中學工作。搭配由外師錄製的「即答力MP3」，聽、說、讀三管齊下

嚴選字彙 　近400個餐飲關鍵字彙+應用例句

必備句型 　精選192句餐飲從業人員必備句，各有3種不同的說法，近600種的變化

附「即答力」MP3

Food and Beverage

F & B

English

作者教授餐飲英文、觀光餐旅英文多年。這本「**一本搞定內外場餐飲英語**」涵蓋外場服務工作內容，包含餐廳訂位、餐桌擺設、餐廳帶位、點餐服務、飲料服務、餐間服務、處理客訴、餐後結帳，與宴會服務。關於內場食材處理 – 蔬菜與水果、湯品、主菜，與甜點相關對話也有詳盡的解說。

本書共有 12 個 unit，每個 unit 都依主題有四個相關對話，每個對話後有這個對話裡八個重要必學的單字與例句。所有例句都是與餐飲內外場工作內容有關。讀者可藉由這些例句學習到更多職場上會用到的句子。在例句之後作者於每個對話中挑選出四個重要句子，列出每個句子兩種不同說法。讀者可藉由換句話說了解英文溝通上不同的表述方法。熟讀本書，相信您會具備餐飲業職場上所需的英語會話能力，對求職與升遷都會有莫大的幫助。

王郁琪

根據萬事達卡在 2015 年所發佈的「全球最佳旅遊城市報告」中指出，在全世界的 132 個城市所做的統計，「旅客年成長率」的排名當中，台北的排名高居全球第一，而在「旅客平均消費」的項目當中，國際觀光客在台北的花費平均為 4 萬 2500 元，為全世界排名第 3。

有鑑於近幾年來，台灣在國際觀光這一部分的吸金能力，連帶著餐飲等的相關行業也蓬勃發展，尤其是在針對國際觀光客的服務需求大量的增加，餐飲英語便成了相當熱門的學習項目。而本書中將餐飲英語以內場（廚房區域）及外場（服務區域）作為分類，一本就涵括了餐飲業的完整風貌。對於無論是需要做內外場 cross training 的餐飲業管理階層、常需要與外籍旅客直接交談的服務人員、有外籍上司的內場廚師亦或是想一窺餐飲職場完整流程的大眾都適合閱讀本書。書中有用簡單的基礎英文再加上餐飲職場的專業用語，讓您一讀就會，再加上專業外籍老師所錄製的對話 mp3，邊讀邊聽邊說，有助於迅速提高英語「即答力」，創造出激增的顧客滿意度，也進階的獲得主管的賞識，增加自我的「薪動力」！

編輯部

Contents 目次

Part 1 Serving Area 外場

Part 2　Cooking Area
內場

Part 1

Serving Area

外場

Unit 01

Reservation
餐廳訂位

1.1

We are fully booked on that day.
訂位已滿

 Dialogue 停不住對話 🎧01

H ▶ Host 領檯　**G** ▶ Guest 客人

H ▶ Good afternoon, you have reached Ponderosa Steakhouse. This is Angus speaking, how may I help you?

領檯 ▶ 午安,龐德羅莎牛排。我是Angus,有什麼可以為您服務的?

G ▶ <u>I am wondering if your restaurant accepts reservations.</u>

客人 ▶ 請問你們餐廳接受訂位嗎?

H ▶ Yes, we do.

領檯 ▶ 有的。

G ▶ That's great. Then I'd like to reserve a table for six o'clock this Friday night, please.

客人 ▶ 那太好了。我想要訂本週五晚六點的位子。

H ▶ I'm afraid we're fully booked at 6 p.m. on that day, but we have a table available at 7 p.m. Is the time suitable for you?

領檯 ▶ 那天晚上六點的位子恐怕已經訂滿了，但我們七點還有位子。這個時間合適嗎？

G ▶ OK, it's fine.

客人 ▶ 好的，可以。

H ▶ Thanks for your understanding, Miss. May I have your name and contact number, please?

領檯 ▶ 小姐，謝謝您的諒解。請問您貴姓大名和聯絡電話？

G ▶ It's Alice Lin. You can reach me on my cell phone. My number is 0987654321.

客人 ▶ 我是Alice Lin。你可以打我手機。我的電話是0987654321。

H ▶ Thank you, Ms. Lin. How many people will there be in your party?

領檯 ▶ 謝謝您，林小姐。你們一行幾個人？

G ▶ There will be five of us, three adults and two kids.

客人 ▶ 我們五個人，三個大人兩個小孩。

H ▶ Yes, Ms. Lin. Do you need high chairs and tableware for children?

領檯 ▶ 是的，林小姐。你需要兒童餐椅和餐具嗎？

G ▶ Yes, please. Thanks for asking.

客人 ▶ 需要，謝謝您的

By the way, could I reserve a private room?

H ▶ I am afraid not. <u>Our private rooms are for a party over 8. We are sorry about that.</u>

G ▶ That's OK. Then could I have a table near the window in the main dining area?

H ▶ No problem. Your reservation is done. I've reserved a table under your name, for three adults and two kids, at 7 p.m. this Friday, the fifth of July.

G ▶ That's correct, thank you.

H ▶ Thanks for calling. We look forward to seeing you this Friday.

詢問。順道一提,我可以訂包廂嗎?

領檯 ▶ 恐怕不行。我們的包廂是8個人以上才能訂的,很抱歉。

客人 ▶ 沒關係。那我可以訂在主餐區靠窗的位子嗎?

領檯 ▶ 沒問題。您的訂位已經完成。我已用您的名字訂了本週五七月五號晚上七點的位子,三大兩小。

客人 ▶ 正確,謝謝。

領檯 ▶ 謝謝您的來電。期待在本週五和您見面。

Vocabulary 字彙

1. **accept** [ək`sɛpt] **vt** 及物動詞　接受，領受；答應，同意
   At our restaurant, we don't accept any drunk guests.
   在我們餐廳，我們不接受任何喝醉酒的客人。

2. **reservation** [ˌrɛzɚ`veʃən] **n** 名詞　預訂
   You can call us back three days in advance to confirm your reservation.
   你可以在三天前打電話給我們以確認您的預訂。

3. **suitable** [`sutəb!] **adj** 形容詞　適當的；合適的；適宜的
   We have a private room available on that day that is suitable for you to throw a birthday party.
   我們那天有一個包廂適合你們辦生日派對。

4. **contact** [`kɑntækt] **n** 名詞 / **v** 動詞　聯絡 / 與……聯繫
   Can you leave your contact information and we will contact you a.s.a.p. when we find your wallet.
   可以留下您的聯絡訊息嗎？當我們找到您的皮夾時我們會盡快與您聯繫。

5. **tableware** [`teb!ˌwɛr] **n** 名詞　（總稱）餐具
   We provide a set of good–looking, heat–resistant, and all-plastic tableware.
   我們提供一套美觀，耐熱的全塑餐具。

6. **private** [`praɪvɪt] **adj** 形容詞　個人的，私人的
   We are told not to discuss clients' private matters.
   我們被告知不能討論客人的私人事務。

7.**main** [men] adj 形容詞　主要的，最重要的

Main courses are half price from 1pm to 2pm on Mondays and Wednesdays this month.

這個月每週三和五主菜在中午一點到兩點間是半價。

8.**correct** [kə`rɛkt] adj 形容詞　正確的

The chef told me to add some vinegar to make a correct seasoning.

主廚叫我加點醋把味道調好。

In Other Words 這樣說也能通

1. I am wondering if your restaurant accepts reservations.

請問你們餐廳接受訂位嗎？

✧ Does your restaurant accept reservations?

✧ May I make a reservation?

2. I'm afraid we're fully booked at 6 p.m. on that day.

那天晚上六點的位子恐怕已經訂滿了。

✧ I'm afraid we don't have any table available at 6 p.m. on that day.

✧ We are sorry that there is no table available at 6 p.m. on that day.

3. How many people will there be in your party?

你們一行幾個人？

✧ How big is your party?

✧ How many are there in your party?

4. Our private rooms are for a party over 8. We are sorry about that.

我們的包廂是8個人以上才能訂的，很抱歉。

✧ We are sorry that you can reserve a private room only when you have more than 8 people.

✧ Our private rooms can only be rented to groups of at least 8 people.

Unit 01

Reservation
餐廳訂位

There won't be any tables available tonight. 今天晚上已經沒有位子了

 Dialogue 停不住對話

H ▶ Host 領檯 G ▶ Guest 客人

H ▶ Good morning. Little Sheep Hotpot. Mike speaking. Is there anything I can help you with?

領檯 ▶ 早安。小肥羊火鍋。我是Mike。有什麼可以為您服務的？

G ▶ Yes, I'd like to book a table for 4 this evening.

客人 ▶ 是的，我想訂今晚四個人的位子。

H ▶ I'm very sorry, Ma'am. There won't be any tables available tonight.

領檯 ▶ 非常抱歉，女士。今天晚上已經沒有位子了。

G ▶ Oh, my god, why is the restaurant fully booked today?

客人 ▶ 天啊，今天餐廳怎麼這麼滿？

H ▶ Actually we are fully booked almost every day in the winter time. I strongly recommend that you make a reservation one week in advance next time.

領檯 ▶ 事實上冬天我們每天幾乎都客滿。我強烈建議您下次在一週前就要預先訂位。

G ▶ It's such a pity that we can't have your hotpot tonight.

客人 ▶ 真可惜我們今晚不能吃你們的火鍋了。

H ▶ We have one new branch on Roosevelt Rd. Do you mind going there? I am sure they still have tables available tonight. They serve the same hotpots as we do. I believe you will enjoy the food there as well. In addition, since the branch just opened one month ago, there will be no 10% service charge until next month.

領檯 ▶ 我們在羅斯福路上有一家新的分店。您介意去那嗎？我確定他們今晚還有位子。他們提供和我們一樣的火鍋。我相信您也會很喜歡他們的餐點。除此之外，因為這家分店上個月才開，一直到下個月都不會收10%服務費。

G ▶ That sounds nice. I would like to give it a try. I wonder where the restaurant is. Is it far from your restaurant?

客人 ▶ 聽起來很棒。我會想試試看。請問餐廳在哪？離你們餐廳很遠嗎？

H ▶ Don't worry. It's not far and you can just take the MRT and get off at Taipower Building station. Our branch

領檯 ▶ 別擔心。那沒有很遠，您可以搭捷運，在台電大樓站下車。我

01 Unit
02 Unit
03 Unit
04 Unit
05 Unit
06 Unit
07 Unit
08 Unit

is right next to Exit 3. It will take you about 20 minutes to get there from here.

G ▶ Good. Could you give me their number and I can call them to reserve a table.

H ▶ It's 02-26845623. I'm sorry about the inconvenience. I hope we can serve you next time.

G ▶ No problem. <u>Thanks very much for your help and suggestion.</u>

H ▶ My pleasure.

們的分店就在三號出口旁。從我們餐廳到那裡大概只要**20**分鐘。

客人 ▶ 很好。你可以給我他們的電話嗎,我可以打電話去訂位。

領檯 ▶ 電話是02-2684-5623。希望下次有機會為您服務。

客人 ▶ 沒關係。非常謝謝你的幫助和建議。

領檯 ▶ 我的榮幸。

Vocabulary 字彙

1. **recommend** [ˌrɛkə`mɛnd] **vt** 及物動詞　推薦，介紹
Can you recommend the popular dishes in your restaurant?
你可以推薦你們餐廳受歡迎的菜餚嗎？

2. **in advance** [ɪnəd`væns] **ph** 片語　預先
Our restaurant is so famous and popular that guests have to make reservations up to two months in advance in order to dine here on Christmas Eve.
我們餐廳非常有名與受歡迎，客人必須提前兩個月預訂才能在平安夜當天在此用餐。

3. **pity** [`pɪtɪ] **n** 名詞　可惜的事，憾事
What a pity that we are closed for renovation during this period of time. Do you mind calling us back in the beginning of next month?
真可惜我們在這段期間因重新裝潢歇業中。您介意下個月初再來電嗎？

4. **branch** [bræntʃ] **n** [C] 可數名詞　分公司；分店；分局；分部；部門
We opened a local branch in Kaohsiung this month.
這個月我們在高雄開了一家分店。

5. **mind** [maɪnd] **vt** 及物動詞　（用於否定句和疑問句中）介意，反對
I am sorry that our apple pies are sold out today. Do you mind trying our another popular dessert－Fruit Tart?
我很抱歉今天我們的蘋果派都賣完了。您介意試試我們另一個受歡迎的甜點－水果塔嗎？

01 Unit
02 Unit
03 Unit
04 Unit
05 Unit
06 Unit
07 Unit
08 Unit

6. **charge** [tʃɑrdʒ]　**n** 名詞　費用，價錢，索價
In Taiwan, most restaurants add a 10 per cent service charge.
在台灣多數餐館加收10%服務費。

7. **suggestion** [sə`dʒɛstʃən]　**n** 名詞　建議
Good evening, sir. I am your waiter tonight. Do you need any suggestion about what to order?
先生，晚安。我是您今晚的服務生。您在點餐方面需要任何建議嗎？

8. **pleasure** [`plɛʒɚ]　**n** 名詞　愉快，高興；滿足
It's my pleasure to serve you tonight.
今晚為您服務是我的榮幸。

In Other Words 這樣說也能通

1. I strongly recommend that you make a reservation one week in advance next time.

   我強烈建議下次記得一週前就要預先訂位。

   ☆ My advice is next time you reserve a table one week in advance.

   ☆ I suggest you make an early reservation, say one week in advance.

2. There will be no 10% service charge until next month.

   直到下個月都不會有10%服務費。

   ☆ We won't charge 10% service fee until next month.

   ☆ You don't need to pay the 10% service fee until next month.

3. I wonder where the restaurant is.

   請問餐廳在哪？

   ☆ May I ask where the restaurant is?

   ☆ Can you tell me where the restaurant is?

4. Thanks very much for your help and suggestion.

   非常謝謝你的幫助和建議。

   ☆ I appreciate for your help and suggestion.

   ☆ I am grateful for your help and suggestion.

01 Unit

02 Unit

03 Unit

04 Unit

05 Unit

06 Unit

07 Unit

08 Unit

Unit 01

Reservation
餐廳訂位

1.3

Could I change my reservation?
我可以更改預約嗎

Dialogue 停不住對話

H ▶ Hostess 領檯　**G** ▶ Guest 客人

H ▶ Good afternoon, Hard Rock Café Xinyi branch, this is Claire, how may I help you?

領檯▶午　安，Hard Rock Café信義店。我是Claire，有什麼能為您服務的嗎？

G ▶ Hi, <u>could I change my reservation?</u>

客人▶是，我可以更改我的預訂嗎？

H ▶ Certainly, sir. <u>Would you please tell me what date your reservation is?</u>

領檯▶當然可以。你可以告訴我您的訂位是哪一天嗎？

G ▶ This Friday. | 客人 ▶ 這個禮拜五。

H ▶ And your name, please? | 領檯 ▶ 請問尊姓大名？

G ▶ Frank Chen. | 客人 ▶ Frank Chen.

H ▶ Thank you, Mr. Chen. I'll check your reservation details, please hold. | 領檯 ▶ 謝謝您，陳先生。我先查一下您的訂位，請稍等。

G ▶ Sure. | 客人 ▶ 好的。

H ▶ I'm sorry to keep you waiting, Mr. Chen. Your reservation was a table for twelve in a private room at 8 o'clock this Friday evening. | 領檯 ▶ 陳先生，很抱歉讓您等候。您預訂的是本週五晚八點在包廂12人的位子。

G ▶ That's correct, but now I'd like to change the scheduled date. | 客人 ▶ 是的。但我現在想改日期。

H ▶ No problem. What date would you like to change it to? | 領檯 ▶ 沒問題，您想要改到哪一天？

G ▶ I'd like to change it to this Saturday, the thirteenth of December. | 客人 ▶ 我想改到這個星期六，12月13日。

H ▶ I'm sorry, Mr. Chen. There are no private rooms left on Saturday night, but we do have tables available in our outdoor garden area. Believe me, this area offers our guests a completely | 領檯 ▶ 陳先生，很抱歉。週六晚上已經沒有包廂的位子了。但在我們的戶外花園區還有位子。相信我，這個區提

<u>different dining atmosphere.</u>　供我們的客人一個完全不同的用餐氣氛。

G ▶ Ok, that's fine.　客人 ▶ 好的，可以。

H ▶ Thank you, Mr. Chen, and the reservation time remains at 8 p.m.?　領檯 ▶ 謝謝您，陳先生。預約時間維持在晚間八點？

G ▶ That's right.　客人 ▶ 是的。

H ▶ How about the number of guests? <u>You still have a party of twelve?</u>　領檯 ▶ 人數呢？一樣是十二位？

G ▶ Oh, I forgot to tell you that there will be only eight people in our party. Thanks for asking.　客人 ▶ 啊，我忘記告訴妳現在只有八位。謝謝妳的詢問。

H ▶ You're welcome. So, I have changed your reservation for a table for eight in the outdoor garden area at 8 p.m. this Saturday. Is that correct?　領檯 ▶ 沒關係。所以，我現在把你的預訂改為本週六晚間八點在戶外花園區的八人位子。正確嗎？

G ▶ Yes, that's right.　客人 ▶ 是的。

H ▶ Thank you for calling. We look forward to seeing you this Saturday.　領檯 ▶ 謝謝您的來電。期待在本週六和您見面。

Vocabulary 字彙

1. **detail** [`ditel]　**n** 名詞　細節
Being a good waiter/waitress requires skills and an eye for details.
作為一個好的服務生需要技巧與注意細節。

2. **private room** [`praɪvɪtrum]　**n** 名詞　包廂
If possible, we'd like a table in a private room.

3. **schedule** [`skɛdʒʊl]　**vt** 及物動詞　安排，預定
Our new branch is scheduled to open later this year.
我們的新分店預計於今年晚些開始營業。

4. **available** [ə`veləb!]　**adj** 形容詞　可用的，在手邊的；可利用的
You will find a wide variety of choices available in our buffet.
在我們的自助餐裡你會發現有很多飲食可供選擇。

5. **guest** [gɛst]　**n** [C] 可數名詞　客人，賓客
You are our honored guests, and I hope you have had a wonderful time dinning here.
您們是我的貴客，希望您們在我這裡用餐愉快。

6. **completely** [kəm`plitlɪ]　**adv** 副詞　完整地；完全地；徹底地
All of our food products are completely natural.
我們所有的食品都是完全天然的。

7. **dining** [`daɪnɪŋ] ⓝ 名詞　用餐

Our dining room has lakeside views and offers excellent cuisine.

我們餐廳有湖邊景色與美味佳餚。

8. **atmosphere** [`ætməsˌfɪr] ⓝ 名詞　氣氛；氛圍

The interior of our banquet hall has an atmosphere of elegance.

我們宴會廳的內部裝潢有著優雅的氛圍。

In Other Words 這樣說也能通

1. Could I change my reservation?

   我可以更改我的預訂嗎？

   ☆ I am wondering if I can change my reservation.
   ☆ Could I make some changes on my reservation?

2. Would you please tell me what date your reservation is?

   你可以告訴我您的訂位是哪一天嗎？

   ☆ May I ask what date your reservation is?
   ☆ What date is your reservation?

3. This area offers our guests a completely different dining atmosphere.

   這個區提供我們的客人一個完全不同的用餐氣氛。

   ☆ Our guests feel completely different when dining in this area.
   ☆ According to our guests, this area offers a completely different dining atmosphere.

4. You still have a party of twelve?

   一樣是十二位？（口語中以疑問口氣而省略倒裝的疑問句）

   ☆ Are there still twelve people in your party?
   ☆ The reservation is still for a party of twelve?

Unit 01

Reservation
餐廳訂位

1.4

I wonder if you can answer some of my questions. 我想請教一些事

 Dialogue 停不住對話

H ▶ Host 領檯　**G** ▶ Guest 客人

H ▶ Daniel French Restaurant. How may I help you?

領檯 ▶ Daniel法式餐廳。有什麼可以為您服務的？

G ▶ Hello. This is Tina Ricks. I made a reservation earlier, and I wonder if you can answer some of my questions.

客人 ▶ 你好，我是 Tina Ricks。我之前已預訂，現在有幾個問題不知你是否可回答我？

H ▶ Sure. I will try my best.

領檯 ▶ 當然，我會盡我所能。

G ▶ Since I am going to celebrate my son's birthday at your restaurant, I am thinking to bring a bottle of my son's favorite white wine with me. <u>Do you charge a corkage fee?</u>

客人 ▶ 因為我會在你們餐廳慶祝我兒子的生日，我想帶一瓶我兒子最喜歡的白酒去。你們會收開瓶費嗎？

H ▶ Yes, we do, but as far as I know it's only a small fee. Let me check with our wine steward now, please hold a minute.

領檯 ▶ 是的，我們收。但就我所知只是一個小額費用。我跟我們的酒侍確認一下，請稍後。

G ▶ No problem.

客人 ▶ 沒問題。

H ▶ Sorry to keep you waiting. The corkage fee is $300 per bottle.

領檯 ▶ 抱歉讓您等待。開瓶費是每瓶三百元。

G ▶ OK. The fee is reasonable.

客人 ▶ 好的，費用合理。

H ▶ In addition, do you need to order a birthday cake at our bakery? <u>Our bakery offers the best birthday cakes in town!</u>

領檯 ▶ 另外，您有需要在我們的烘焙坊預訂生日蛋糕嗎？我們烘焙坊的生日蛋糕在鎮上是最好的喔！

G ▶ Yeah, I've heard that your cakes are very popular. But my husband has ordered a birthday cake

客人 ▶ 我有聽說你們的蛋糕很受歡迎。但我先生已從別的地方訂了生

01 Unit
02 Unit
03 Unit
04 Unit
05 Unit
06 Unit
07 Unit
08 Unit

elsewhere. We are planning to bring that cake with us. Could you put it in the refrigerator when we arrive and have the waiter bring it out to us after the meal?

日蛋糕。我們計畫帶蛋糕過去,你可以在我們抵達時幫我們把蛋糕放在冰箱,然後在用餐後請服務生拿出來給我們嗎?

H ▸ Absolutely.

領檯 ▸ 當然可以。

G ▸ One more thing. <u>My daughter doesn't eat meat</u>. Do you provide vegetarian options?

客人 ▸ 還有一件事。我女兒不吃肉。你們有供應素食嗎?

H ▸ Yes, we have. <u>We offer a vegetarian set menu</u>.

領檯 ▸ 是的,我們有素食套餐菜單。

G ▸ That's great.

客人 ▸ 太好了。

H ▸ Is there anything else I can help you with?

領檯 ▸ 還有什麼能為您服務的嗎?

G ▸ No, thanks. You have been very helpful.

客人 ▸ 不用了,謝謝。你已幫了我很多忙。

H ▸ My pleasure.

領檯 ▸ 我的榮幸。

Vocabulary 字彙

01
Unit

02
Unit

03
Unit

04
Unit

05
Unit

06
Unit

07
Unit

08
Unit

1.**celebrate** [`sɛlə͵bret] **V** 動詞　慶祝
Our restaurant can help our guests organize parties to celebrate birthdays, anniversaries, and so on.
我們餐廳可以幫忙客人安排派對慶祝生日、紀念日等。

2.**bottle** [`bɑt!] **n** 名詞　一瓶的容量
If you need to order meals or a bottle of wine, just call our room service.
如果您需要點餐或一瓶酒，直接打我們的客房服務部。

3.**corkage fee** [`kɔrkɪdʒfi] **n** 名詞　開瓶費
The corkage fee per bottle is NT $ 500 for wines and NT $ 1000 for spirits.
開瓶費紅白酒每瓶台幣500元，烈酒每瓶台幣1000元。

4.**wine steward** [waɪn`stjuwɚd] **n** 名詞　酒侍
Do you mind if I ask the wine steward to serve you some drink first?
我先請酒侍給您上點飲料好嗎？

5.**bakery** [`bekərɪ] **n** 名詞　烘焙坊
In December, our bakery produced 50 percent more bread than we normally did.
我們的烘焙坊12月份製作的麵包比平時多50%。

6.**absolutely** [`æbsə͵lutlɪ] **adv** 副詞　絕對地，完全地
It was absolutely the tastiest food I have ever had.
這絕對是我吃過最好吃的食物。

7.**vegetarian** [ˌvɛdʒəˈtɛrɪən] adj 形容詞　吃素的；素菜的
This is a vegetarian dish that carnivores love.
這是一道肉食主義者愛吃的素菜。

8.**set menu** [sɛtˈmɛnju] n 名詞　套餐菜單
At lunchtime, there's a choice between the buffet and the set menu.
午餐時段可以選擇自助餐或套餐。

In Other Words 這樣說也能通

1. Do you charge a corkage fee?

你們會收開瓶費嗎？

☆ Do I have to pay the corkage fee?

☆ Is there any corkage fee at your restaurant?

2. Our bakery offers the best birthday cakes in town!

我們烘焙坊的生日蛋糕在鎮上是最好的喔！

☆ The birthday cakes at our bakery are one of the best in town.

☆ We are proud to say that our birthday cakes are the best in town.

3. My daughter doesn't eat meat.

我女兒不吃肉。

☆ My daughter is a vegetarian.

☆ My daughter lives on a vegetarian diet.

4. We offer a vegetarian set menu.

我們有素食套餐菜單。

☆ You can order vegetarian set menu here.

☆ There is a vegetarian set menu here.

Unit 02

Table Setting
餐桌擺設

2.1 **Setting a table is easy.** 餐桌擺設很容易

 Dialogue 停不住對話 05

H ▶ Helen 海倫 **T** ▶ Tom 湯姆

H ▶ Hi, Tom. I am Helen. <u>I am new to this job as a server here. The manager asked me to come to you and learn how to set a table.</u>

海倫▶嗨，Tom。 我是Helen。我是新來的服務生。店經理叫我來找你並學習餐桌擺設。

T ▶ No problem. Setting a table is easy. I will show you. First, <u>you have to place the fork to the left of the plate and the knife to the right.</u>

湯姆▶沒問題。餐桌擺設很容易。我做給妳看。首先，妳必須把叉子放在盤子的左邊，刀子放在盤子的右手邊。

H ▶ OK, let me do it. Wait a second. Which way should the blade face?

海倫 ▶ 好的，讓我試試看。等一下，刀面要朝哪一邊？

T ▶ The blade should face inward.

湯姆 ▶ 刀面要朝內。

H ▶ Got it. Also should the fork tines be placed upward or downward?

海倫 ▶ 知道了。叉子要朝上還是朝下？

T ▶ Upward, please.

湯姆 ▶ 請朝上。

H ▶ Done! Then what's next?

海倫 ▶ 放好了。接下來呢？

T ▶ The bread plate must be placed to the left of the fork, but please make sure that you line up the bottom edge with the top of the service plate.

湯姆 ▶ 麵包盤必須放在叉子的左邊，但請確認麵包盤的底線對齊服務盤的上緣。

H ▶ Yes, sir. And I guess I should place the butter knife on the right edge of the bread plate, too, right?

海倫 ▶ 好的！然後我猜我應該把奶油刀放在麵包盤的右邊邊緣，對嗎？

T ▶ That's correct! <u>I can tell you are a quick learner!</u>

湯姆 ▶ 正確！看得出來妳學習能力很強。

H ▶ Thank you. I am flattered.

海倫 ▶ 謝謝。我受寵若驚。

T ▶ Now let's put the red wine glass.

湯姆 ▶ 現在我們來擺放

01 Unit
02 Unit
03 Unit
04 Unit
05 Unit
06 Unit
07 Unit
08 Unit

We place it about 1 inch above the tip of the knife.

紅酒杯。我們放在刀子上方大約一英吋處。

H ▶ OK. How about the water glass?

海倫 ▶ 好的。那水杯呢？

T ▶ The water glass should be set to the left of the red wine glass.

湯姆 ▶ 水杯應該放在紅酒杯的左邊。

H ▶ Got it. I think we are pretty much done.

海倫 ▶ 知道了。我想我們做的差不多了。

T ▶ Yes, please put the napkin on the service plate, and we are done!

湯姆 ▶ 是的，請把餐巾放在服務盤上，然後我們就完成了。

Vocabulary 字彙

1. **blade** [bled] **n** 名詞　刀身，刀片
The blade of this knife is too dull to cut a radish. We should buy a new one.
這把刀太鈍了，無法切蘿蔔，我們應該買一個新的。

2. **face** [fes] **v** 動詞　面對
As a waiter, I have to face many different types of customers every day.
作為一個服務生，我每天都必須面對不同種類的客人。

3. **inward** [`ɪnwɚd] **adv** 副詞　向內
You should shift the plate a bit forward and the knife a little more inward。
你應該把盤子往外挪一點，餐刀往內挪一點。

4. **bottom** [`bɑtəm] **n** 名詞　底部
We have to wait until bubbles are rising from the bottom of the boiling water.
我們必須等到水泡從沸水的底部昇到水面。

5. **edge** [ɛdʒ] **n** 名詞
Don't put the glass near the edge of the table.
不要把玻璃杯放在桌子的邊緣。

6. **place** [ples] **v** 動詞　放置
Would you please place one candlestick on each table?
你可以在每一張桌上都放一個燭台嗎？

01 Unit
02 Unit
03 Unit
04 Unit
05 Unit
06 Unit
07 Unit
08 Unit

7. **flattered** ['flætəd] adj 形容詞　受寵若驚的

I am flattered by the nicest compliment I have ever had .

我感到受寵若驚，這是我聽過最好的讚美。

8. **napkin** [`næpkɪn] n 名詞　餐巾

I will mop up the mess with the napkin.

我會用餐巾很快地將這些亂七八糟的擦乾淨。

In Other Words 這樣說也能通

1. I am new to this job as a server here.
   我是新來的服務生。
   - ✯ I am a new waitress here.
   - ✯ I am new here as a server.

2. The manager asked me to come to you and learn how to set a table.
   店經理叫我來找你並學習餐桌擺設。
   - ✯ The store manager said I can learn how to set a table from you.
   - ✯ The store manager said you will teach me how to set a table.

3. You have to place the fork to the left of the plate and the knife to the right.
   你必須把叉子放在盤子的左邊，刀子放在盤子的右手邊。
   - ✯ The fork should be placed to the left of the plate and the knife to the right.
   - ✯ The fork should be at the left of the plate and the knife at the right.

4. I can tell you are a quick learner!
   看得出來你學習能力很強。
   - ✯ I can tell you learn fast.
   - ✯ I can see that you are a fast learner!

01 Unit
02 Unit
03 Unit
04 Unit
05 Unit
06 Unit
07 Unit
08 Unit

Unit 02

Table Setting
餐桌擺設

2.2

Can you set a table for one person in the formal western style? 你可以擺設正式的一人用西式餐桌嗎

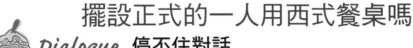

Dialogue 停不住對話 ● 06

M ▶ Manager 經理　**J** ▶ Judy 茱蒂
S ▶ Sandy 珊蒂　**K** ▶ Kevin 凱文

M ▶ Today we will go over how to set a table, and Judy has <u>volunteered to demonstrate for us.</u> Thank you, Judy.

經理 ▶ 今天我們會教大家餐桌擺設。Judy自願幫大家示範。謝謝妳，茱蒂。

J ▶ You're welcome, it's my pleasure.

茱蒂 ▶ 不客氣，我的榮幸。

M ▶ Judy, can you set the table for

經理 ▶ 茱蒂, 妳可以擺

one person in the formal western style? Here are the silverware, glassware, and chinaware.

設正式的一人用西式餐桌嗎？這裡有銀器，玻璃器皿，及瓷器。

J ▶ No problem. First, fold the napkin and place it on the plate. Then put the dinner knife to the right of the napkin. <u>Remember, the blade must face inwards.</u>

茱蒂 ▶ 沒問題。首先，摺好餐巾並放置在盤子上。然後把主餐刀放在餐巾的右邊。記住，刀面要朝內。

M ▶ Yes, that's a good reminder. Please continue.

經理 ▶ 是的，很好的提醒。請繼續。

J ▶ Yes, then you put the dinner fork to the left of the napkin and the bread plate should be placed to the left of the fork. Finally, please put the butter knife on the bread plate. And don't forget to place the handle on the right side and the blade facing down.

茱蒂 ▶ 是，然後把主餐叉放在餐巾的左邊。麵包盤應該放在叉子的左邊。最後，請把奶油刀放在麵包盤上。不要忘記要將把手放在右邊，刀面要朝下。

M ▶ Very good. Judy, please tell everybody about the glassware.

經理 ▶ 很好。茱蒂，接下來請告訴大家如何擺放玻璃器皿。

J ▶ Yes, we place the red wine glass on top of the dinner knife. Then the water goblet should be placed to the left, slightly above the red wine glass. The white wine glass, on the other hand, is placed to the right, slightly

茱蒂 ▶ 是的，我們把紅酒杯放在主餐刀的上方，然後水杯要放在主餐刀的左邊，稍微在紅酒杯的上方。另一方面白酒杯要放在紅酒杯的

01 Unit
02 Unit
03 Unit
04 Unit
05 Unit
06 Unit
07 Unit
08 Unit

below the red wine glass. | 下面一點點。

M ▶ The table is almost set. Do you have any questions so far? | 經理 ▶ 餐桌擺設快完成了。到目前為止你們有任何問題嗎？

Sandy raises her hand. | 珊蒂舉手

S ▶ How about the salt and pepper shakers? Should we put them in the middle of the table? | 珊蒂 ▶ 鹽和胡椒罐呢？我們應該把它們放在桌子中央嗎？

J ▶ Good question! Yes, you are right. | 茱蒂 ▶ 好問題。是的，妳是對的。

Kevin raises his hand. | 凱文舉手

K ▶ What do we use to decorate the table? | 凱文 ▶ 那我們要用什麼布置餐桌？

J ▶ We usually decorate the tables with flowers. | 茱蒂 ▶ 我們通常用新鮮花卉布置餐桌。

M ▶ Any other questions? If no, let's give Judy a big hand! | 經理 ▶ 還有其他問題嗎？如果沒有，讓我們給茱蒂大大的掌聲。

J ▶ Thank you, everyone. | 茱蒂 ▶ 謝謝各位。

Vocabulary 字彙

1. **volunteer** [ˌvɑlən`tɪr] **v** 動詞 自願（做）； n 名詞 自願者
Can I have a volunteer to wash the dishes?
誰自願來幫忙洗一下碗？

2. **silverware** [`sɪlvɚˌwɛr] **n** 名詞 銀餐具
We will ensure a sufficient supply of all silverware, glassware, and chinaware for service.
我們會確認供應足夠的餐具，杯子，和瓷器。

3. **glassware** [`glæsˌwɛr] **n** 名詞 玻璃器皿
Our kitchen assistant made sure that the glassware was always spotlessly clean.
我們的廚房助理總是把玻璃器皿洗得乾淨光亮。

4. **chinaware** [`tʃaɪnəˌwɛr] **n** 名詞 陶瓷器
All our chinaware was rimmed with gold.
我們所有的陶瓷餐具都鑲有金邊。

5. **goblet** [`gɑblɪt] **n** 名詞 高腳杯；（無柄）酒杯
One goblet of red wine and one bottle of beer, please.
請給我一杯紅酒和一罐啤酒。

6. **slightly** [`slaɪtlɪ] **adj** 形容詞 輕微地；稍微地
The meat is slightly charred.
肉有點焦了。

7.**middle** [ˋmɪd!]   adj 形容詞   中間的（可表位置或時間）；中等的
I am afraid she can't help you now because she is in the middle
of cleaning those tables.
她現在恐怕沒辦法幫你因為她正在清理那些桌子。

8.**decorate** [ˋdɛkəˏret]   v 動詞   裝飾
I will decorate these semi-finished cakes with some cream.
我會用奶油裝飾這些半成品蛋糕。

In Other Words 這樣說也能通

01
Unit

02
Unit

03
Unit

04
Unit

05
Unit

06
Unit

07
Unit

08
Unit

1. Today we will go over how to set a table, and Judy has volunteered to demonstrate for us.

今天我們會教大家餐桌擺設。Judy自願幫大家示範。

✯ Today we will teach you how to set a table, and Judy is the volunteer to demonstrate for us.

✯ Today we will go through table setting, and Judy will voluntarily demonstrate for us.

2. Remember, the blade must face inwards.

記住，刀面要朝內。

✯ Please remember to make the blade face in.

✯ Don't forget that the knife's blade should always point toward the plate.

3. The table is almost set.

餐桌擺設快完成了。

✯ We are 99% done with the table setting.

✯ We have almost finished table setting.

4. Let's give Judy a big hand!

讓我們給Judy大大的掌聲。

✯ Let's give Judy a big applause.

✯ Let's thank Judy with enthusiastic applause.

Unit 02

Table Setting
餐桌擺設

2.3

I only have less than twenty minutes left. 我只剩不到20分鐘

 Dialogue 停不住對話　　　　　　　

M ▶ Mandy　曼蒂　　**B** ▶ Billy　比利

M ▶ Would you please help me set these two tables? The dinner party will begin at 6:30 p.m. I only have less than twenty minutes left.

曼蒂 ▶ 可以請你幫我把最後這兩個餐桌擺設好嗎？晚餐宴會六點半就要開始。我只剩不到20分鐘。

B ▶ Gosh! <u>You should have asked me for help earlier.</u> How many guests are you expecting tonight?

比利 ▶ 天啊！妳應該早點請我幫忙。今晚妳有幾位客人？

M ▸ Three for table 9 and four for table 11.

曼蒂 ▸ 九號桌三位，十一號桌四位。

B ▸ Ok, I will spread the tablecloths first.

比利 ▸ 好的，我先鋪桌巾。

M ▸ Thank you so much for your help.

曼蒂 ▸ 非常謝謝你的幫忙。

B ▸ You're welcome! What dishes for these two tables?

比利 ▸ 不客氣！今天這兩桌的菜是什麼？

M ▸ Let me check. Table 9 ordered a Radish Cake, a Sweet and Sour Fish, a Honey Ham, and a Stir Fry Cabbage, and I will serve table 11 with a Cantonese Fried Rice, a Cashew Nuts Shrimp, a Lemon Chicken, and a Scrambled Egg.

曼蒂 ▸ 讓我確認一下。九號桌點了蘿蔔糕、糖醋魚、蜜汁火腿、炒高麗菜。十一桌的菜是港式炒飯、腰果蝦、檸檬雞、和炒蛋。

B ▸ Then <u>a Chinese place setting should be fine for both tables.</u>

比利 ▸ 這樣兩桌都用中式擺設就可以了。

M ▸ Yes, I think so. I will put chopsticks and chopstick rests on table 9. Would you please do so to the table 11?

曼蒂 ▸ 是的，我想也是。我會放九桌的筷子和筷架。你可以幫我放11桌的嗎？

B ▸ No problem. I will put them next to the rice bowls.

比利 ▸ 沒問題。我會把它們放在碗旁邊。

M ▸ Great, thanks.

曼蒂 ▸ 太好了，謝謝。

01 Unit

02 Unit

03 Unit

04 Unit

05 Unit

06 Unit

07 Unit

08 Unit

B ▸ By the way, are you going to serve soup for these two tables?

M ▸ Oh, thanks for reminding me. Both tables ordered soups. <u>Table 9 is chicken soup, and table 11 is pork ribs broth.</u>

B ▸ Then <u>you have to prepare soup spoons and small bowls for your guests.</u>

M ▸ You are right. I will go get 7 spoons and 7 small bowls now.

B ▸ Go ahead. In the meanwhile, I will put the salt and pepper shakers along with soy sauce and vinegar on the table.

M ▸ Thank you, Billy.

比利 ▸ 對了，兩桌有要上湯嗎？

曼蒂 ▸ 喔，謝謝你的提醒。兩桌都有點湯。九桌點雞湯，十一桌點排骨湯。

比利 ▸ 這樣妳必須幫客人準備喝湯的湯匙和小碗。

曼蒂 ▸ 你是對的。我現在就去拿七個湯匙和七個小碗。

比利 ▸ 去吧。我現在把鹽巴和胡椒罐、醬油和醋放在桌上。

曼蒂 ▸ 謝謝你，比利.

Vocabulary 字彙

1. **spread** [sprɛd] ☑ 動詞 張開;展開;攤開
   Please spread the onion slices on the bottom of the dish.
   請把洋蔥片鋪在菜盤底部。

2. **tablecloth** [ˋtebl͵klɔθ] ⋒ 名詞 桌布
   The guest at Table 9 knocked his teacup over, and the tea went all over the tablecloth.
   第九桌的客人把茶杯打翻了,撒的桌布上到處都是。

3. **radish** [ˋrædɪʃ] ⋒ 名詞 蘿蔔
   It is sliced pork and radish soup with pepper powder. It's Sichuan style.
   這是加了胡椒粉的蘿蔔肉片湯,四川風味。

4. **scramble** [ˋskræmbl] ☑ 動詞 【美】炒(蛋)
   Would you like our chef to scramble some eggs with onions for you?
   你想要主廚幫你用洋蔥炒些蛋嗎?

5. **chopsticks** [ˋtʃɑp͵stɪks] ⋒ 名詞 筷子
   That guest is not very skillful with his chopsticks. You might have to offer him a fork.
   那位客人用筷子不太熟練,你可能需要給他叉子。

6. **rib** [rɪb] ⋒ 名詞 排骨,肋條
   We make our soup with prime rib and various vegetables.
   我們用上等排骨和多種蔬菜煮湯。

7. **broth** [brɔθ] **n** 名詞　（用肉、蔬菜等煮成的清淡的）湯
I like this chicken broth. May I have some more?
我喜歡這個雞湯，我可以再喝一點嗎？

8. **vinegar** [`vɪnɪgɚ] **n** 名詞　醋
If the sauce seems too sweet, you can add some red wine vinegar.
如果醬汁太甜，你可以加些紅酒醋。

In Other Words 這樣說也能通

1. You should have asked me for help earlier.

妳應該早點請我幫忙。

☆ Why didn't you ask me for help earlier?

☆ You should have asked me to help you earlier.

2. A Chinese place setting should be fine for both tables.

兩桌都用中式擺設就可以了。

☆ I think we will set both tables in the Chinese way.

☆ I think both tables should be set in the Chinese way.

3. Table 9 is chicken soup, and table11 is pork ribs broth.

九桌點雞湯，十一桌點的是排骨湯。

☆ Table 9 ordered chicken soup and I will serve table 11 pork ribs broth.

☆ I will serve chicken soup, and ribs broth for table 9 and 11 respectively.

4. You have to prepare soup spoons and small bowls for your guests.

妳必須幫客人準備喝湯的湯匙和小碗。

☆ Your guests should have soup spoons and small bowls.

☆ You have to serve your guests soup spoons and small bowls.

Unit 02
Table Setting
餐桌擺設

2.4 I was wondering what the service plate is for? 服務盤是做什麼用的？

 Dialogue 停不住對話　　　　　08

H ▸ Hanny 漢妮　**V** ▸ Victor 維克多

H ▸ Vic, I have some questions about the table setting.

漢妮 ▸ 維克，我有一些關於餐桌擺設的問題。

V ▸ One of my responsibilities is teaching you how to set a table. So, just go ahead.

維克多 ▸ 我的職責之一就是教你如何擺設餐桌。所以，就直接問吧！

H ▸ Thank you. First of all, I am quite confused about the service plate.

漢妮 ▸ 謝謝你，首先，我對服務盤感到很困

01
Unit

02
Unit

03
Unit

04
Unit

05
Unit

06
Unit

07
Unit

08
Unit

Where should I put it on the table?

惑。我應該把它放在桌上哪裡？

V ▸ We usually lay the service plate about one inch from the table edge.

維克多 ▸ 我們通常把服務盤放在離桌沿一英吋的地方。

H ▸ I see. Like this?

漢妮 ▸ 我知道了。像這樣？

V ▸ Yes, you did it right.

維克多 ▸ 是的，妳做對了。

H ▸ I was wondering what the service plate is for?

漢妮 ▸ 我想知道服務盤是做什麼用的？

V ▸ Actually it only has ornamental function and the guest won't use it.

維克多 ▸ 事實上它只有裝飾功能，客人不使用它。

H ▸ Wow, I didn't know that. Now that the service plate is for ornamental use only, I will leave it on the table and I don't need to take it away. Am I right?

漢妮 ▸ 哇，原來如此。既然服務盤只有裝飾功能，我就一直放在桌上不需要拿走它。對嗎？

V ▸ No, you should take the service plate away before the first course is served. Or you can leave it until the main course is brought out.

維克多 ▸ 不，你應該在送第一道菜之前把服務盤收走。或者你可以在送上主菜後收走它。

H ▶ Thank you. How about the napkins? Should they be placed on top of the dinner plate or on the side plate?

漢妮 ▶ 謝謝你。那餐巾呢？它們應該被放在主餐盤還是邊盤的上面？

V ▶ Either way is fine, but we usually put them on the dinner plate.

維克多 ▶ 都可以。但我們通常放在主餐盤上。

H ▶ Got you! One final question. <u>How do you memorize where to place different plates, forks, and spoons?</u> I found it quite difficult.

漢妮 ▶ 知道了！最後一個問題。你如何記住不同的盤子、叉子，和湯匙該放在哪裡？我覺得很難記。

V ▶ It's not difficult at all. Even though the amounts and styles of the utensils are depended on the served meals, you can make things easier by memorizing just one rule. Remember to place the utensils in the order of serving, from the outside in. This will cause less confusion for both you and your guests.

維克多 ▶ 一點都不難。即使餐具的數量和種類取決於不同的餐點，你可以靠著只記住一個規則來簡化事情。記住，餐具擺放的位置依據出餐的順序從外擺到內。這可以幫你和你的客人減輕很多困惑。

Vocabulary 字彙

01
Unit

02
Unit

03
Unit

04
Unit

05
Unit

06
Unit

07
Unit

08
Unit

1. **lay** [le] **v** 動詞　放，擱
You have to lay the hotpot in the center of the table.
你必須把火鍋放置在桌子的正中央。

2. **ornamental** [ˌɔrnəˈmɛnt!] **adj** 形容詞　裝飾的；作裝飾用的
These ornamental service plates are so pretty.
這些裝飾用的服務盤好漂亮。

3. **course** [kors] **n** 名詞　一道菜
Today's combo is a six-course meal.
今天的套餐含六道菜。

4. **memorize** [ˈmɛməˌraɪz] **v** 動詞　記住；背熟
As a waiter, you have to memorize all the dishes we offer in this restaurant.
作為一個服務生，你必須牢記我們餐廳的每一道菜。

5. **spoons** [spun] **n** 名詞　湯匙
The spoon slipped out of my hand. Can you give me another one?
湯匙從我手中滑落。你可以再給我一個嗎？

6. **utensil** [juˈtɛns!] **n** 名詞　器皿，用具
Our kitchen uses stainless steel cooking utensils because they are durable.
我們廚房用不銹鋼炊具，因為比較耐用。

7.**order** [`ɔrdɚ] **n** 名詞　順序，次序

Can you list all the guests who are coming tonight in alphabetical order?

你可以把今晚要來的所有客人名單按照字母排列嗎？

8.**confusion** [kən`fjuʒən] **n** 名詞　混淆，困惑

This misprint in the menu led to great confusion among our guests.

菜單印刷錯誤造成我們客人很大的困惑。

In Other Words 這樣說也能通

1. I have some questions about table setting.

我有一些關於餐桌擺設的問題。

⭐ May I ask you something about table setting?

⭐ Could you answer some of my questions regarding table setting?

2. Actually, it only has ornamental function.

事實上它只有裝飾功能。

⭐ In fact it's only for ornamental purposes.

⭐ Actually, we use it only for decorative purposes.

3. You can leave it until the main course is brought out.

你可以在送上主菜後收走它。

⭐ You can take it away once the main course is brought out.

⭐ You don't need to take it away until the main course is served.

4. How do you memorize where to place different plates, forks, and spoons?

你如何記住不同的盤子、叉子，和湯匙該放在哪裡？

⭐ How do you memorize where different plates, forks, and spoons should be?

⭐ Can you tell me how you memorize where to put different plates, forks, and spoons?

Unit 03

Guest receptions
餐廳帶位

3.1

Seating Customers. 帶位

 Dialogue 停不住對話

H ▶ Hostess 領檯　**T** ▶ Tina 蒂娜　**G** ▶ Gloria 葛洛莉

H ▶ Good evening. Welcome to Ponderosa Steakhouse. Do you have a reservation?

領檯 ▶ 晚安。歡迎來到龐德羅莎牛排館。您有訂位嗎？

T ▶ Yes, we've booked a table for two at 7:30 p.m.

蒂娜 ▶ 有的，我們訂了晚上7:30分兩人的位子。

H ▶ Whose name was the reservation made under?

領檯 ▶ 請問訂位大名是？

G ▸ It's mine. Gloria Lin.

葛洛莉 ▸ 是我。Gloria Lin。

H ▸ Thanks. Let me check your reservation now. Yes, you have made a reservation for 7:30 this evening. We have arranged a table for you near the window with a nice night view. Please follow me.

領檯 ▸ 謝謝。讓我確認您的訂位。是的，您訂了今晚7:30分的位子。我們為您們安排了靠窗有很好夜景的位子。請跟我來。

T ▸ Thank you.

蒂娜 ▸ 謝謝。

H ▸ Please have a seat. Is this table all right?

領檯 ▸ 請坐。這個位子OK嗎？

G ▸ Definitely. The night view is really nice. I like it.

葛洛莉 ▸ 當然。這裡的夜景真的很讚。我喜歡。

H ▸ Have you been to our restaurant before?

領檯 ▸ 您們有來過我們餐廳嗎？

G ▸ Yes, I have dined here about two months ago. I was impressed with your rib eye steaks and that's why I brought my friend here today.

葛洛莉 ▸ 有的，兩個月前我在這裡用過餐。我對你們的肋眼牛排印象深刻，所以我今天帶我朋友來吃。

H ▸ Glad to hear that you enjoyed our steak. Your waitress tonight will be Candy. She will be here soon to take your order. This month we have

領檯 ▸ 很高興知道你喜歡我們的牛排。今晚您們的服務生是Candy。她馬上會來幫您們點

several new appetizers and desserts and Candy will talk to you about them. I hope you'll enjoy the dinner tonight.

餐。這個月我們有幾個新的開胃菜和甜點，Candy 待會為跟您們介紹。希望您們喜歡今晚的晚餐。

G ▶ Thank you, sir.

葛洛莉 ▶ 先生，謝謝您。

H ▶ Would you like anything to drink while you wait? We offer a list of non-alcoholic drinks such as sodas, fruit juice, and coffee.

領檯 ▶ 等待的時間有要點飲料嗎？我們有無酒精的飲料例如汽水，果汁，和咖啡。

T ▶ May I have some hot tea, please?

蒂娜 ▶ 你們有熱茶嗎？

H ▶ Sure, how about English rose tea?

領檯 ▶ 當然，英式玫瑰茶可以嗎？

T ▶ Great. We will have two cups of hot tea for now.

蒂娜 ▶ 太好了。我們現在來兩杯熱茶。

H ▶ Certainly.

領檯 ▶ 沒問題。

Vocabulary 字彙

01
Unit

02
Unit

03
Unit

04
Unit

05
Unit

06
Unit

07
Unit

08
Unit

1. **arrange** [ə`rendʒ] **vt** 及物動詞　安排；籌備[+to-v][+that][+wh-]
We have arranged a private room for you.
我們幫您準備了包廂的位子。

2. **follow** [`fɑlo] **vt** 及物動詞　跟隨
You go first, and I will follow.
你先去，我隨後就來。

3. **definitely** [`dɛfənɪtlɪ] **adv** 副詞　肯定地；當然
I will definitely arrive on time, just stop worrying.
我一定準時到，你放心就是了。

4. **dine** [daɪn] **v** 動詞　進餐；用餐
Do you dine out much?
你常常在外用餐嗎？

5. **impressed** [ɪm`prɛsd] **adj** 形容詞　對～印象深刻
Many guests are impressed with our soup of the day. I highly recommend it.
很多客人都對我們的例湯印象深刻。我極力推薦。

6. **appetizer** [`æpə͵taɪzɚ] **n** 名詞　開胃菜
Small savory biscuits provide a simple appetizer.
美味可口的小餅乾就是簡單的開胃品。

7. **dessert** [dɪˋzɝt]　**n** 名詞　飯後甜點
Would you like some dessert now, miss?
現在要來點甜品嗎，小姐？

8. **non-alcoholic** [nanˌælkəˋhɔlɪk]　**adj** 形容詞　不含酒精的
Can I have something non-alcoholic?
給我來杯不含酒精的飲料好嗎？

In Other Words 這樣說也能通

1. We have arranged a table for you near the window with a nice night view.

我們為您們安排了靠窗有很好夜景的位子。

✯ Your table is near the window, and therefore you can enjoy the nice night view. I hope you will like it.

✯ Your table today is near the window with a nice night view. I hope you will enjoy it.

2. Have you been to our restaurant before?

您們有來過我們餐廳嗎？

✯ Is this your first time to dine here?

✯ Have you ever been to our restaurant?

3. I was impressed with your rib eye steaks.

我對你們的肋眼牛排印象深刻。

✯ I like your rib eye steak very much.

✯ Your rib eye steak impressed me a lot.

4. Glad to hear that you enjoyed our steak.

很高興知道你喜歡我們的牛排。

✯ I am pleased to know that you enjoyed our steak.

✯ I'm happy to know that you like our steak.

01 Unit
02 Unit
03 Unit
04 Unit
05 Unit
06 Unit
07 Unit
08 Unit

Unit 03

Guest receptions
餐廳帶位

3.2

Waiting to be seated. 等待帶位

 Dialogue 停不住對話 (10)

H ▶ Hostess 領檯　**K ▶ Kevin** 凱文

H ▶ Good evening, sir. Welcome to Little Sheep Hotpot. Do you have a reservation?

領檯 ▶ 先生，晚安。歡迎來到小肥羊火鍋。您有訂位嗎？

K ▶ Sorry, I don't. Is there a table available now?

凱文 ▶ 抱歉，我沒有。你們現在有位子嗎？

H ▶ <u>Unfortunately, we are fully seated at the moment.</u> I am sorry that you will have to wait.

領檯 ▶ 很遺憾我們現在是客滿的。很抱歉你需要等喔。

K ▶ <u>Will that be a long wait?</u>　　凱文 ▶ 要等很久嗎？

H ▶ May I ask how many people there are in your party, please?　　領檯 ▶ 可以請問您們幾位嗎？

K ▶ A table for 4, please. My friends are coming in about ten minutes.　　凱文 ▶ 請給我四人的位子。我朋友們十分鐘內會到。

H ▶ Let me check the waiting list. There are five groups ahead of you on the waiting list.　　領檯 ▶ 我看一下等待名單。在名單上有五組人排在你們前面。

K ▶ So, you mean there will be a long wait before a table is available?　　凱文 ▶ 所以，你的意思是要等很久才有位子？

H ▶ I am afraid so. You might have to wait for about one hour.　　領檯 ▶ 恐怕是如此。您可能要等大約一小時。

K ▶ OK, I think we will just wait.　　凱文 ▶ 好的，我們會等。

H ▶ <u>Thanks for your patience</u>, sir. Now I'll put you on the waiting list. May I have your name and mobile phone number, please?　　領檯 ▶ 謝謝您的耐心，先生。現在您已在等待名單上。可以給我您的大名和手機號碼嗎？

K ▶ Sure, it's Kevin Lamb, and my number is 0987654321.　　凱文 ▶ 當　然。Kevin Lamb。我的手機號碼是0987654321。

H ▶ OK, thanks. <u>We'll call you when</u>　　領檯 ▶ 好的，謝謝。有

01 Unit

02 Unit

03 Unit

04 Unit

05 Unit

06 Unit

07 Unit

08 Unit

<u>your table is ready.</u> Do you want to have a seat in our reception area while waiting?

您的位子時我會打電話給您。您要在接待區坐著等待嗎？

K ▶ Thanks for asking, but I think my friends and I will go window shopping at the department store nearby.

凱文 ▶ 謝謝，但我和朋友會去附近的百貨公司逛逛。

H ▶ Sounds like a good idea. I hope a table will be ready quicker than expected.

領檯 ▶ 聽起來是不錯的主意。希望能比預期更快給您位子。

K ▶ Me too. See you later.

凱文 ▶ 我也希望。待會見。

H ▶ See ya.

領檯 ▶ 待會見。

Vocabulary 字彙

1. **unfortunately** [ʌn`fɔrtʃənɪtlɪ] adv 副詞　遺憾地；可惜
Unfortunately, we don't offer seafood dishes today.
很遺憾我們今天沒有海鮮菜餚。

2. **fully** [`fʊlɪ] adv 副詞　完全地；徹底地
Although it was off-season, our hotel was fully occupied.
雖然現在是淡季，我們飯店還是客滿的。

3. **seated** [`sitɪd] adj 形容詞　就座的
Six people or more can be seated comfortably at this table.
這張桌子可以很舒服地坐六個人以上。

4. **ahead** [ə`hɛd] adv 副詞　在前
We labored hard to finish our job ahead of schedule.
我們努力工作以期在表定時程前完成工作。

5. **afraid** [ə`fred] adj 形容詞　（用於提出異議，告訴不好的消息等場合，使語氣婉轉）恐怕，遺憾 [+（that）]
We don't have anything like that, I'm afraid.
我們恐怕沒有那樣的東西。

6. **patience** [`peʃəns] n 名詞　耐心；忍耐；耐性；毅力
We would like to thank you for your patience and understanding.
我們要感謝您的耐心和理解。

7.**reception** [rɪ`sɛpʃən]   **n** 名詞　接待

Our restaurant recently did the catering for a presidential reception.

我們餐廳最近承辦了一次總統招待會的宴席。

8.**expected** [ɪk`spɛktɪd]   **adj** 形容詞　期待中的

The demand to dine in our restaurant is much greater than expected.

要來我們餐廳用餐的需求大大超過預期。

In Other Words 這樣說也能通

01
Unit

02
Unit

03
Unit

04
Unit

05
Unit

06
Unit

07
Unit

08
Unit

1. Unfortunately, we are fully seated at the moment.

很遺憾我們現在是客滿的。

✬ I am sorry that we are fully occupied now.

✬ I'm afraid that we don't have any table available now.

2. Will that be a long wait?

要等很久嗎？

✬ Do I have to wait for a long time?

✬ Am I going to wait for long?

3. Thanks for your patience, sir.

謝謝您的耐心，先生。

✬ I am grateful for your patience, sir.

✬ Thank you for being patient, sir.

4. We'll call you when your table is ready.

有您的位子時我會打電話給您。

✬ We'll give you a call when your table opens up.

✬ We'll ring you once your table is ready.

Unit 03

Guest receptions
餐廳帶位

3.3 ## The walk-in guest. 沒有預約的客人

 Dialogue 停不住對話 🎧11

H ▶ Host 領檯　S ▶ Susan 蘇珊

H ▶ Good evening, miss, and welcome to the Sunrise Café. Have you made a reservation?

領檯 ▶ 小姐晚安。歡迎來 到Sunrise Café。請問有訂位嗎？

S ▶ Sorry, I haven't. Do you have a table available now?

蘇珊 ▶ 抱歉，沒有。你們現在有位子嗎？

H ▶ Yes, we do. You don't have to wait! We can seat you <u>immediately</u>.

領檯 ▶ 有的，您不用等待，我們可以馬上帶您入座。

S ▸ That's great.

領檯 ▸ 太好了。

H ▸ May I ask how many people are there in your party?

領檯 ▸ 請問幾位用餐？

S ▸ A total of five, and <u>I am expecting the other four to be here any minute now.</u>

蘇珊 ▸ 總共五位，包含我自己。我想其他四位很快就會到了。

H ▸ No problem. Would you prefer a seat in the main dining area or at the bar?

領檯 ▸ 沒問題。您想要坐在主餐區還是吧檯？

S ▸ <u>That would be nice if you can give me a table in the main dining area.</u>

蘇珊 ▸ 如果你可以給我主餐區的位子就太好了。

H ▸ Sure, this way, please.

領檯 ▸ 當然，這邊請。

Susan is seated.

蘇珊已就坐。

H ▸ May I bring you a glass of water while you are waiting for your friends to come?

領檯 ▸ 您在等朋友來時需要我給您上杯水嗎？

S ▸ Do you offer any soft drinks?

蘇珊 ▸ 您們有提供軟性飲料嗎？

H ▸ Yes, we do. Here's our soft drink list. Please take a look.

領檯 ▸ 有的，我們的飲料單就在桌上，請看一下。

01 Unit
02 Unit
03 Unit
04 Unit
05 Unit
06 Unit
07 Unit
08 Unit

S ▶ I would like to have a glass of fresh squeezed pineapple juice, thank you.

蘇珊 ▶ 我想點一杯新鮮現榨鳳梨汁，謝謝。

H ▶ Certainly. I will be right back with your juice.

領檯 ▶ 沒問題，馬上為您準備果汁送上來。

The host is back with the pineapple juice.

領檯員送上果汁。

H ▶ Here you are, Miss.

領檯 ▶ 小姐，您的果汁。

S ▶ Thank you.

蘇珊 ▶ 謝謝。

H ▶ Since we are the best live music restaurant in Taipei. Every Friday, which is today, is what we called the live music night. <u>Tonight we have a very popular band</u> coming to perform classical Jazz music.

領檯 ▶ 因為我們是全台北市最棒的有現場演奏的餐廳，每週五，也就是今天，我們有現場演奏夜。今晚我們有非常受歡迎的樂團來演奏經典爵士樂。

S ▶ Woo, I didn't know that. We are so lucky to be here today. We all like Jazz music very much!

蘇珊 ▶ 哇，我不知道呢！我們真幸運今天來這。我們都很喜歡爵士樂。

Vocabulary 字彙

1. **immediately** [ɪ`midɪtlɪ] adv 副詞　立即，即刻，馬上
Your waitress will be here immediately to take your order.
你的服務生會立即過來幫你點餐。

2. **dining** [`daɪnɪŋ] n 名詞　用餐
I checked the seating arrangements before the guests filed into the dining-room.
我在客人陸續進入餐廳之前核對了一遍座位安排。

3. **bar** [bɑr] n 名詞　吧檯
Perhaps while you wait you would like a drink at the bar.
也許在您等待時，您可以在吧檯點東西喝。

4. **squeeze** [skwiz] vt 及物動詞　榨，擠，壓，擰
This machine helps you to squeeze more juice out.
這台機器能擠出更多的果汁。

5. **popular** [`pɑpjələ] adj 形容詞　受歡迎的
The sweet-sour chicken is one of the most popular dishes in our restaurant.
甜酸雞是我們餐廳最受歡迎的菜色之一。

6. **band** [bænd] n 名詞　樂團
The band continued with their set after a short break.
樂團在短暫休息後繼續演奏他們的曲目。

7. **perform** [pə`fɔrm] **v** 動詞　演出，執行，完成

I believe I can perform the tasks assigned to a waiter.

我相信我可以完成指派給服務生的任務。

8. **classical** [`klæsɪk!] **adj** 形容詞　古典的

People dining in our restaurant can enjoy both the delicious food and classical music.

在我們餐廳用餐的人可以享受美味食物和古典音樂。

In Other Words 這樣說也能通

1. We can seat you immediately.

我們可以馬上帶您入座。

☆ You can have a table immediately.

☆ You will have a seat right away.

2. I am expecting the other four to be here any minute now.

我想其他四位很快就會到了。

☆ I think the other four will be here soon.

☆ The other four are coming and will arrive soon.

3. That would be nice if you can give me a table in the main dining area.

如果你可以給我主餐區的位子就太好了。

☆ I would like to have a table in the main dining area, thank you.

☆ I would prefer to sit in the main dining area, thank you.

4. Tonight we have a very popular band coming to perform classical Jazz music.

今晚我們有非常受歡迎的樂團來演奏經典爵士樂。

☆ Tonight all our guests can enjoy classical Jazz music played by a popular band.

☆ Tonight a very popular band will come to perform classical Jazz music at our restaurant.

Unit 03

Guest receptions
餐廳帶位

3.4 **Can I get a different table?** 我可以換位子嗎

 Dialogue 停不住對話 🎧12

W ▸ Waiter 服務生　**G** ▸ Gina 吉娜

W ▸ Good evening. Do you have a reservation?

服務生 ▸ 晚安。請問有訂位嗎？

G ▸ Yes, I do. I made the reservation one week ago. My name is Gina Lin.

吉娜 ▸ 有的。我一週前訂的位。我的名字是 Gina Lin.

W ▸ Yes. We have been expecting you to come. Please come this way. Here is your table.

服務生 ▸ 是的，我們正等候您的光臨。請這邊走。這是您的位子。

G ▶ The table is too close to the washroom. Can I get a different one?

吉娜 ▶ 這的位子太靠近洗手間。我可以換一個嗎？

W ▶ Sorry about that. Let me arrange another one for you. <u>Is that table in the corner all right for you?</u>

服務生 ▶ 很抱歉。讓我安排另一個位子給您。角落那個位子可以嗎？

G ▶ Yes, that would be fine.

吉娜 ▶ 好的，角落的位子可以。

W ▶ Follow me, please. Here is the menu. <u>Would you care for something to drink first?</u>

服務生 ▶ 請跟我來。這是您的菜單。要先點飲料嗎？

G ▶ Yes, I'd like a beer. Can you tell me what brands you have?

吉娜 ▶ 好的，我想點啤酒。你可以告訴我你們有哪些牌子嗎？

W ▶ Sure, my pleasure. We have Taiwan beer, which is very popular. If you prefer an imported beer, <u>we also have a wide range of imported beers to choose from</u> such as Heineken, Budweiser, and Suntory.

服務生 ▶ 當然，這是我的榮幸。我們有非常受歡迎的台灣啤酒。如果你喜歡進口啤酒，我們也有多種進口啤酒可供選擇例如海尼根、百威、和三得利。

G ▶ I'll take Suntory. I like Japanese beers very much.

吉娜 ▶ 我要點三得利。我非常喜歡日本啤酒。

W ▶ No problem. Can or bottle?

服務生 ▶ 沒問題。您要罐裝還是瓶裝的？

G ▸ Bottle, please.

吉娜 ▸ 請給我瓶裝的。

W ▸ Miss Lin, you have reserved a table for four. When can I expect the other three to come?

服務生 ▸ 林小姐，您訂了四人的位子。請問其他三位何時會到？

G ▸ A table for four? No, I thought you knew that I am a single guest.

吉娜 ▸ 四人的位子？我以為你們知道我是單獨客人。

W ▸ That's ok. There must have been some mistake occurred. It's our fault. Sorry about that.

服務生 ▸ 沒關係，一定是有一些錯誤。這是我們的錯，很抱歉。

G ▸ Never mind. By the way, I am a vegetarian. Do you have a vegetarian menu?

吉娜 ▸ 沒關係。對了，我吃素，請問你們有素食菜單嗎？

W ▸ Certainly. We have some very popular vegetarian dishes here. Your waiter tonight is Sam. He will be with you in a minute to introduce those dishes to you.

服務生 ▸ 當然。我們有一些非常受歡迎的素食菜餚。您今晚的服務生是Sam。他馬上會過來跟您介紹。

Vocabulary 字彙

1. **washroom** [`wɑʃˌrum] **n** 名詞 洗手間
Can you show me the way to the washroom?
你能告訴我哪裡是洗手間嗎？

2. **corner** [`kɔrnɚ] **n** 名詞 角落
That guest requested a table at the corner rather than the one near the washroom.
那位客人要求在角落的位子而不是靠近洗手間的位子。

3. **import** [`ɪmport] **v** 動詞 進口
Since our restaurant provides authentic Korean food, we imported most of the ingredients from Korea.
因為我們餐廳提供正宗的韓式料理，我們大部分的食材從韓國進口。

4. **can** [kæn] **n** 名詞 罐裝
We never use canned food, and we prepare every dish by using fresh and natural food.
我們從不用罐裝食物，我們用新鮮自然的食材準備每一道菜。

5. **bottle** [`bɑt!] **n** 名詞 瓶裝
We offer a variety of non-alcoholic drinks and bottle water.
我們提供多樣的非酒精性飲料和瓶裝水。

6. **single** [`sɪŋ!] **adj** 形容詞 單一的；單獨的
We aim to provide the best customer service to every single guest.
我們致力於提供每一位客人最好的客戶服務。

7.**occur** [ə`kɝ]　**vi** 不及物動詞　發生
I hope this won't occur again.
我希望這種事不要再發生一次。

8.**fault** [fɔlt]　**n** 名詞　錯誤
I was disappointed whenever the cook found fault with my work.
每當廚師挑剔我的工作時，我都非常沮喪。

In Other Words 這樣說也能通

1. Is that table in the corner all right for you?

   角落那個位子可以嗎？

   ⭐ Do you mind if I arrange the table in the corner for you?

   ⭐ Do you mind to sit in the corner?

2. Would you care for something to drink first?

   要先點飲料嗎？

   ⭐ Would you like to order a drink first?

   ⭐ Do you want something to drink now?

3. We also have a wide range of imported beers to choose from.

   我們也有多種進口啤酒可供選擇。

   ⭐ We provide a variety of imported beers for you to choose.

   ⭐ You can choose many different kinds of beers offered here.

4. Miss Lin, you have reserved a table for four.

   林小姐，您訂了四人的位子。

   ⭐ Miss Lin, your reservation shows that you have a party of four.

   ⭐ Miss Lin, you have a party of four coming.

Unit 04

Ordering
點餐服務

Questions about the menu.有關菜單的問題

 Dialogue 停不住對話 🎧13

W ▶ Waiter 服務生　**V** ▶ Victor 維克多　**S** ▶ Susan 蘇珊

W ▶ Good evening. I am your waiter for this evening. My name is Alexander. You can just call me Alex. May I take your order now?

服務生 ▶ 晚安。我是您們今晚的服務生。我的名字是Alexander。你叫我Alex就好。現在可以幫您點餐了嗎？

V ▶ Umm… I don't think we're ready yet. <u>There are some dishes on the menu that we have no idea what they are.</u>

維克多 ▶ 嗯……我想我們還沒準備好。這個菜單上的某些菜我們完全不知道是什麼。

W ▶ Don't worry, sir. I am here to explain the menu to you and I will do my best to answer your questions. First of all, what kind of food do you prefer?

V ▶ My wife and I would like to try some local Taiwanese food, and we know that Squid Pottage is famous. However, we have no clue what that is.

W ▶ Yes, Squid Pottage is one of our most popular dishes. It comes with a pot of squid meat, Chinese mushroom, bamboo shoots, and some eggs. It is soup based, but you can add noodles or rice in it.

S ▶ It sounds delicious and nutritious. Honey, should we order one with noodles?

V ▶ Why not?

W ▶ OK, I will ask our chef to make a pot for two people. Besides, I recommend Sweet and Sour Pork Chops. Many of our guests said it's a must-eat dish at our restaurant.

服務生 ▶先生，別擔心。我現在就跟您們解釋菜單，我也會盡力回答您們的問題。首先，您們偏好何種食物？

維克多 ▶我太太和我想吃吃看台灣小吃，我們聽說魷魚羹很有名。但是我們完全不知道那是什麼。

服務生 ▶是的，魷魚羹是我們的招牌菜之一。它有一鍋的魷魚、香菇、筍絲、還有一些蛋。它有湯底，但你可以選擇加飯或麵在裡面。

蘇珊 ▶聽起來很美味也很營養。親愛的，我們要不要選加麵的？

維克多 ▶好啊。

服務生 ▶好的，我會請我們主廚做一鍋兩人份的。除此之外，我推薦糖醋豬排。我們很多客人都說這是我們餐廳必點的一道菜。

V ▸ OK, we will try that as well.

維克多 ▸ 我們也試試看。

S ▸ Now I guess we'd better order one vegetable dish. What do you have?

蘇珊 ▸ 現在我們最好點一道蔬菜。你們有什麼？

W ▸ You can choose between stir frying and blanching, we have spinach and cabbage.

服務生 ▸ 您們可以選要水煮或是清炒，我們有菠菜及高麗菜。

S ▸ Fried Cabbage, please.

蘇珊 ▸ 請給我們炒高麗菜。

W ▸ No problem, ma'am. Anything else?

服務生 ▸ 沒問題，女士。還要點其他的嗎？

V ▸ No, that's all.

維克多 ▸ 沒有了。

W ▸ Let me repeat your orders. You ordered a pot of Squid Pottage with noodles, one Sweet and Sour Pork Chops and one Fried Cabbage. Is that correct?

服務生 ▸ 讓我重複您們點的菜。您點了魷魚羹麵、糖醋豬排及炒高麗菜。正確嗎？

S ▸ Yes, that's correct. Thank you.

蘇珊 ▸ 是的，正確。謝謝你。

W ▸ You're welcome, and I'll be back with your orders soon.

服務生 ▸ 不客氣，我會儘快將您們點的餐點送上。

Vocabulary 字彙

1. **pottage** [`pɑtɪdʒ] **n** 名詞　濃湯，羹湯
We will serve you a nice of pottage at the beginning.
我們會先為您上一份不錯的濃湯。

2. **pot** [pɑt] **n** 名詞　罐；壺；鍋
Do you have self - service hot pot, please?
你們有自助火鍋嗎？

3. **mushroom** [`mʌʃrʊm] **n** 名詞　蘑菇
We offer several mushroom based dishes, such as cheese and mushroom omelet, a ham and mushroom pizza, and French onion and mushroom soup.
我們提供幾樣以蘑菇為基底的菜餚，包含起司蘑菇蛋捲，火腿蘑菇披薩，和法式洋蔥蘑菇湯。

4. **bamboo** [bæm`bu] **n** 名詞　竹筍
How about pork shreds with bamboo shoots?
來一份竹筍肉絲如何？

5. **noodles** ['nu:dəlz] **n** 名詞　麵條
That guest finished off two bowls of chicken noodles soup in no time.
那個客人很快就吃完兩碗雞湯麵。

6. **nutritious** [nju`trɪʃəs] **adj** 形容詞　有營養的
To help provide essential nourishment, we've put together these nutritious drinks.
為了幫助提供必要的營養，我們調配了這些營養果汁。

01 Unit
02 Unit
03 Unit
04 Unit
05 Unit
06 Unit
07 Unit
08 Unit

7. **chef** [ʃɛf] n 名詞　主廚

I work as an assistant chef at an Italian restaurant.
我在一家義式餐廳擔任助理廚師。

8. **spinach** [`spɪnɪtʃ] n 名詞　菠菜

Spinach, eggplant, cabbage, cauliflower, cucumber and radish are the common vegetables used in our restaurant.
菠菜、茄子、高麗菜、花椰菜、黃瓜和白蘿蔔都是我們餐廳常用的蔬菜。

In Other Words 這樣說也能通

1. There are some dishes on the menu that we have no idea what they are.

這個菜單上的某些菜我們完全不知道是什麼。

⭐ We have no idea about some dishes listed on the menu.

⭐ We don't know anything about some of the dishes on the menu.

2. I am here to explain the menu to you and I will do my best to answer your questions.

我現在就跟您們解釋菜單，我也會盡力回答您們的問題。

⭐ I will try my best to explain the menu to you and answer every question you raise.

⭐ I will explain the menu to you and feel free to ask me any questions.

3. What kind of food do you prefer?

您們偏好何種食物？

⭐ May I ask what type of food you enjoy more?

⭐ What sort of food do you like more?

4. Many of our guests said it's a must-eat dish at our restaurant.

我們很多客人都說這是我們餐廳必點的一道菜。

⭐ This is a must-eat dish at our restaurant, according to our guests.

⭐ This is our signature dish.（這是我們的招牌菜。）

01 Unit

02 Unit

03 Unit

04 Unit

05 Unit

06 Unit

07 Unit

08 Unit

Unit 04

Ordering

點餐服務

<table>
<tr><td>4.2</td><td><h2>Ordering at a western restaurant. 在西餐廳的點餐</h2></td></tr>
</table>

 Dialogue 停不住對話 🎧14

W ▸ Waiteress 服務生   **G** ▸ Guest 客人

W ▸ May I take your order now?

服務生 ▸ 可以為您點餐了嗎？

G ▸ Yes, we'd like to order the Christmas Special Set Meal.

客人 ▸ 好的，我們想點聖誕套餐。

W ▸ Certainly. <u>Would you like to start with an appetizer?</u>

服務生 ▸ 沒問題，要先點開胃菜嗎？

G ▸ What appetizers do you have?

客人 ▸ 你們有什麼開胃菜？

W ▸ We have Snails in Garlic Butter, Smoked Salmon, and Creamed Tuna on Toast.

服務生 ▸ 我 們 有 烤 田 螺、煙燻鮭魚、鮪魚吐司。

G ▸ I would like a Smoked Salmon, please.

客人 ▸ 我要煙燻鮭魚。

W ▸ Yes, sir. <u>How about soup? We have Chowder, Pumpkin Soup, and French Onion Soup.</u>

服務生 ▸ 好的，先生。湯呢？我們有巧達湯、南瓜湯、法式洋蔥湯。

G ▸ Pumpkin Soup, please.

客人 ▸ 南瓜湯。

W ▸ What main course would you like to order?

服務生 ▸ 您想點什麼主餐？

G ▸ Let me see… you have Sirloin Steak, Fish Fillet, and Roasted Lamb Chops…

客人 ▸ 我看一下……你們有沙朗牛排、魚排、烤羊排……

W ▸ That's correct.

服務生 ▸ 是的。

G ▸ It's hard to decide. <u>What main course do you recommend?</u>

客人 ▸ 很難決定。你推薦什麼主餐？

W ▸ These three main courses are all very popular. What do you like to have for today, beef, fish, or lamb?

服務生 ▸ 這三個主菜都很受歡迎。你今天想吃什麼？牛肉、魚、還是羊肉？

G ▸ OK, I think I'll have the steak.

客人 ▸ 好的，我想我就點牛排。

01 Unit

02 Unit

03 Unit

04 Unit

05 Unit

06 Unit

07 Unit

08 Unit

W ▸ How would you like your steak — Rare, medium, or well done?

服務生 ▸ 您的牛排要幾分熟？三分、五分、還是全熟？

G ▸ Medium, please.

客人 ▸ 五分熟，謝謝。

W ▸ <u>Would you like your steak with a baked potato or French fries?</u>

服務生 ▸ 您的牛排要搭配烤洋芋或薯條？

G ▸ I would prefer French fries, thanks.

客人 ▸ 我點薯條，謝謝。

W ▸ We will serve you a dessert after the main course. What would you like? Fruit Tart, Vanilla Ice Cream, or Cheese Cake?

服務生 ▸ 主餐後會上甜點。您想要水果塔、香草冰淇淋還是起司蛋糕？

G ▸ I heard that your Cheese Cake is very good. I'll go for it.

客人 ▸ 我聽說你們的起司蛋糕很棒。我點起司蛋糕。

W ▸ No problem, sir. Let me repeat your order. You've ordered a Smoked Salmon, a Pumpkin Soup, a medium Sirloin Steak with French fries, and a Cheese Cake.

服務生 ▸ 沒問題，先生。讓我重複您的訂單。您點了煙燻鮭魚、南瓜湯、五分熟沙朗牛排配薯條和起司蛋糕。

G ▸ That's correct. Thank you very much.

客人 ▸ 正確。非常謝謝您。

Vocabulary 字彙

1. **garlic** [`gɑrlɪk] **n** 名詞　大蒜
This dish is served with generous amount of garlic.
這道菜加入大量的蒜。

2. **smoked** [smokt] **adj** 形容詞　煙燻的
Smoked salmon is our signature dish. I highly recommend it.
煙燻鮭魚是我們的招牌菜。我強力推薦。

3. **chowder** [`tʃaʊdə] **n** 名詞　海鮮雜燴濃湯
We serve the chowder with slices of fresh baked bread.
我們的海鮮濃湯有搭配幾片新鮮現烤麵包。

4. **pumpkin** [`pʌmpkɪn] **n** 名詞　南瓜
On Thanksgiving, we offer the American traditional dish, pumpkin pie.
在感恩節當天，我們提供美國傳統菜餚，南瓜派。

5. **fillet** [`fɪlɪt] **n** 名詞　去骨肉切片
Place the sliced pork fillet on top and pour a little sauce over it.
把豬肉片放在上頭，並淋上一點醬料。

6. **roasted** [rost] **adj** 形容詞　烘烤的
Many of our customers are fond of our roasted duck.
我們很多客人都喜歡我們的烤鴨。

7. **dessert** [dɪ`zɝt] **n** 名詞　甜點
I was tempted by the dessert menu.
你們的甜點菜單讓我垂涎欲滴。

8.**vanilla** [vəˈnɪlə] **n** 名詞　香草

Yes, we provide Powdered Sugar, Peanut, Cinnamon, Chocolate, and Vanilla toppings.

是的，我們提供糖粉、花生粉、肉桂粉、巧克力粉，和香草粉。

In Other Words 這樣說也能通

1. Would you like to start with an appetizer?

要先點開胃菜嗎？

⭐ Would you care for an appetizer?

⭐ What would you like to go first, an appetizer?

2. How about soup? We have Chowder, Pumpkin Soup, and French Onion Soup.

湯呢？我們有巧達湯、南瓜湯、法式洋蔥湯。

⭐ What soup would you like to order? We offer a choice of Chowder, Pumpkin Soup, or FrenchOnion Soup.

⭐ Would you like to order a soup? We have three soups to choose from, Chowder, Pumpkin Soup, and French Onion Soup.

3. What main course do you recommend?

您想點什麼主餐？

⭐ Could you give me some suggestions about what main course to order?

⭐ Could you recommend the main course?

4. Would you like your steak with a baked potato or French fries?

您的牛排要搭配烤洋芋或薯條？

⭐ What would you like to go with your steak, a baked potato or French fries?

⭐ Our steak is either with a baked potato or French fries. Which do you like?

Unit 04

Ordering
點餐服務

4.3 **Ordering Chinese dishes.** 在中餐廳的點餐

 Dialogue 停不住對話 🎧15

W ▶ Waiteress 服務生　**G** ▶ Guest 客人

W ▶ Good evening, ma'am. May I get you something to drink while you browse the menu?

服務生 ▶ 晚安，女士。您在看菜單時需要我為您點飲料嗎？

G ▶ OK, we'd like to try some beer. What brand do you have?

客人 ▶ 好的，我們想點啤酒。你們有什麼牌子？

W ▶ We only have Taiwan beer. Taiwan beer is more popular than other brands.

服務生 ▶ 我們只有台灣啤酒。台灣啤酒比其他廠牌受歡迎。

G ▶ I see. We'll take four cans, very cold, please.

客人 ▶ 了解。那我們要點四罐,要很冰的。

W ▶ No problem.

服務生 ▶ 沒問題。

W ▶ Are you ready to order, ma'am?

服務生 ▶ 女士,可以為您點餐了嗎?

G ▶ We are interested in the Diced Chicken with Peanuts in Chili Sauce. Is it spicy? <u>My friends don't eat spicy food.</u>

客人 ▶ 我們想點宮保雞丁。它是辣的嗎?我朋友不吃辣。

W ▶ I'm afraid the Diced Chicken with Peanuts in Chili Sauce is one of our spicy dishes.

服務生 ▶ 不好意思宮保雞丁是辣的喔。

G ▶ Then how about the Drunken Chicken? Can you explain to me what that is?

客人 ▶ 那醉雞呢?你可以跟我解釋那是什麼嗎?

W ▶ It's a very famous dish in Chinese cuisine. The chicken meat was soaked in the rice wine stock. It's tasty and most importantly, it's not hot.

服務生 ▶ 這在中式料理中算是一道名菜。雞肉是浸泡在摻有米酒的高湯中。很美味。最重要的是,它不辣。

G ▶ Great. We'll take the Drunken Chicken. Besides the chicken, we'd like a pork dish, too. What do you recommend?

客人 ▶ 太好了,那我們就點醉雞。除了雞肉外,我們也想點一道豬肉料理。您建議什麼?

01 Unit
02 Unit
03 Unit
04 Unit
05 Unit
06 Unit
07 Unit
08 Unit

W ▶ Many of our guests like our Braised Pork in Soy Sauce a lot.

服務生 ▶ 我們很多客人都喜歡我們的紅燒豬肉。

G ▶ That sounds delicious. I think we'll take it.

客人 ▶ 聽起來很美味。我們點吧。

W ▶ Would you care for some soup? You may turn to the next page where the soups are listed.

服務生 ▶ 您們喜歡喝湯嗎？您可以翻到下一頁，那列出我們所有的湯品。

G ▶ We'd like the Wonton Soup. By the way, do you think we've ordered enough for four people?

客人 ▶ 我們喜歡餛飩湯。順道一提，您覺得我們點的餐點夠四人份嗎？

W ▶ I'd suggest you order two more dishes. You now have one chicken, one pork dish, and one soup. You can consider ordering dishes of beef, seafood, or a vegetable.

服務生 ▶ 我會建議再點兩道。您已經點了一道雞肉，一道豬肉料理，和一份湯品。您可以考慮點牛肉，海鮮和蔬菜料理。

G ▶ I see. A Beef with Tomato and a Steamed Fish, please.

客人 ▶ 我知道了。請幫我點番茄牛肉和清蒸魚。

W ▶ Got it.

服務生 ▶ 收到。

Vocabulary 字彙

01 Unit

02 Unit

03 Unit

04 Unit

05 Unit

06 Unit

07 Unit

08 Unit

1. **brand** [brænd] n 名詞 商標；牌子
We offer the best English brand of tea.
我們有最好品牌的英國茶。

2. **popular** [`pɑpjələ] adj 形容詞 受歡迎的
In summer, our hotel is a hugely popular venue for wedding receptions.
在夏天我們飯店是最受歡迎的婚宴舉辦地。

3. **diced** ['daɪst] adj 形容詞 切成丁的
Our spicy diced chicken with peanuts tastes tender and nice.
我們的宮保雞丁吃起來又嫩又香。

4. **spicy** [`spaɪsɪ] adj 形容詞 辛辣的
The spicy dishes call for red wine rather than white wine.
辛辣的菜餚較適合搭配紅酒而非白酒。

5. **cuisine** [kwɪ`zin] n 名詞 菜餚
All our private rooms have lakeside views and offer excellent cuisine.
我們所有的包廂都可欣賞湖邊景色並提供美味佳餚。

6. **tasty** [`testɪ] adj 形容詞 美味的；可口的
Going veggie can be tasty, easy and healthy too.
吃素也可以很可口，烹調容易，並且有益健康。

7. **consider** [kən`sɪdɚ] **v** 動詞　考慮

Sir, do you still need time to consider what to order?

先生，你還需要時間想想要點什麼餐嗎？

8. **steamed** [stim] **adj** 形容詞　蒸的

We offer Chinese breakfast like steamed buns, eggrolls, and soybean milk.

我們提供中式早餐包含饅頭、蛋餅和豆漿。

In Other Words 這樣說也能通

1. My friends don't eat spicy food.

   我朋友不吃辣。

   ★ My friends don't care for spicy food.

   ★ I'm afraid spicy food is not what my friends want.

2. Many of our guests like our Braised Pork in Soy Sauce a lot.

   我們很多客人都喜歡我們的紅燒豬肉。

   ★ Braised Pork in Soy Sauce is one of our popular dishes.

   ★ Braised Pork in Soy Sauce is very popular among our guests.

3. You may turn to the next page where the soups are listed.

   您可以翻到下一頁，那列出我們所有的湯品。

   ★ All our soups are listed on the next page.

   ★ As for what soup to order, you can refer to the next page.

4. Do you think we've ordered enough for four people?

   您覺得我們點的餐點夠四人份嗎？

   ★ Do you think what we've ordered is enough for four people?

   ★ Are the dishes we ordered so fat enough for four people?

01 Unit / 02 Unit / 03 Unit / 04 Unit / 05 Unit / 06 Unit / 07 Unit / 08 Unit

Unit 04

Ordering
點餐服務

4.4

Did you save room for dessert?
要來些甜點嗎

 Dialogue 停不住對話

W ▶ Waiter 服務生 **G1** ▶ Guest 1 客人1
G2 ▶ Guest 2 客人2

W ▶ Here is our menu. Please take your time.

服務生 ▶ 這是我們的菜單。請慢慢看。

G1 ▶ Do you have a Chef's special today?

客人1 ▶ 你們今天有提供特餐嗎？

W ▶ Yes, we do. Today's special is grilled ribs. Besides, we offer 10% discount on this special set meal only today and tomorrow.

服務生 ▶ 有的。今天的特餐是烤肋排。此外，今明兩天我們的特餐打九折。

G1 ▸ Really?! That's great. What comes with it?

客人1▸真的喔？！太棒了。請問它的副餐是什麼？

W▸We have five side dishes to choose from, rice with green peas, mashed potatoes, boiled carrots, stuffed tomatoes, and mixed salad.

服務生 ▸我們有五種附餐可選擇，青豆飯、馬鈴薯泥、水煮紅蘿蔔、充餡番茄、和混合沙拉。

G1 ▸ I'll have mashed potatoes.

客人1▸我點洋芋泥。

G2 ▸ Mixed salad, please.

客人2▸混和沙拉，謝謝。

W▸What kind of dressing would you like, ma'am?

服務生 ▸小姐，請問您要何種沙拉醬？

G1 ▸ I'll have the Thousand Island dressing.

客人1▸我想要千島醬。

W▸Oh, we are very sorry that we don't have the Thousand Island dressing. We offer vinaigrette, mustard, French, and ranch dressing.

服務生 ▸很抱歉我們沒有千島醬。我們有醋醬、芥末醬、法式沾醬和田園沾醬。

G1 ▸ I will go for vinaigrette.

客人1▸我選醋醬。

W▸Thank you, ma'am. I will be right back with your grilled ribs with your preferred side dishes.

服務生 ▸謝謝，女士。您的烤肋排和您選的副餐馬上來。

W ▶ How was your meal?

服務生 ▶ 您 的 餐 點 如何？

G2 ▶ Really good. My wife and I both enjoyed the grilled ribs very much.

客人2▶非常棒。我太太和我都很喜歡你們的烤肋排。

W ▶ I'm glad to hear that. So, <u>did you two save room for dessert?</u>

服務生 ▶ 很高興聽到您這麼說。請問您現在想來點甜點嗎？

G2 ▶ I am pretty full now and to be honest, I am not a big fan of sweets.

客人2▶我 現 在 很 飽了，而且老實說我不喜歡甜食。

G1 ▶ Unlike him, I do enjoy sweets. Can you recommend something good?

客人1▶不像他，我很喜歡吃甜食。你可以建議好吃的嗎？

W ▶ I am proud to say that we have the best cheesecake in town.

服務生 ▶ 我很驕傲地說我們的起司蛋糕是城內最好的。

G1 ▶ How did you know that cheesecake is my favorite dessert?!

客人1▶你怎麼知道起司蛋糕是我最喜歡吃的甜點？！

W ▶ Then <u>I can ensure you that you will be impressed by our cheesecake and fall in love with it!</u>

服務生 ▶ 這樣我可以跟你保證你會被我們的起司蛋糕深深打動並愛上它。

Vocabulary 字彙

1. **rib** [rɪb]　ⓝ名詞　肋排
Rib meat will be washed and cut into 1.5 cm square block.
肋條肉洗乾淨然後切成1.5公分的塊狀。

2. **mash** [mæʃ]　ⓥ動詞　把……搗成糊狀
Can you pass me one scoop of mashed potato, please?
可以遞給我一球馬鈴薯泥嗎？

3. **boil** [bɔɪl]　ⓥ動詞　水煮
Check every 20 minutes that the water has not boiled away.
每二十分鐘檢查一下以防水都燒乾了。

4. **stuffed** [stʌft]　ⓐⓓⓙ形容詞　塞了餡料的
He stuffed the chicken with garlic, ginger, and spring onion.
他在雞肉裡塞滿了大蒜、薑、和青蔥。

5. **dressing** [ˋdrɛsɪŋ]　ⓝ名詞　（拌沙拉等用的）醬料
Drizzle the remaining dressing over the fried pork chop and salad.
把剩下的醬料淋在炸豬排和沙拉上。

6. **vinaigrette** [ˏvɪnəˋgrɛt]　ⓝ名詞　醋醬
To save calories, we use light vinaigrette or low - calorie Italian dressing.
為了減少卡路里，我們用清淡醋醬和低卡路里的意式沾醬。

01 Unit
02 Unit
03 Unit
04 Unit
05 Unit
06 Unit
07 Unit
08 Unit

7. **sweet** [swit]　**n** 名詞　甜食

Do you eat sweets, cakes or sugary snacks?

你吃糖果、蛋糕、或甜點嗎？

8. **ensure** [ɪnˋʃʊr]　**v** 動詞　保證；確保

We ensure every one of our customers who dine in our restaurant receive the best customer service.

我們確保每一位到我們餐廳用餐的客人都有最好的客戶服務。

In Other Words 這樣說也能通

1. We offer 10% discount on this special set meal only today and tomorrow.

今明兩天我們的特餐打九折。

✰ You will get 10% discount on the special set meal you order only today and tomorrow.

✰ On today and tomorrow, we offer 10% discount on this special set meal.

2. What kind of dressing would you like, ma'am?

小姐，請問您要何種沾醬？

✰ Would you like to choose the dressing, ma'am?

✰ What dressing do you prefer, ma'am?

3. Did you two save room for dessert?

請問您現在想來點甜點嗎？

✰ Would you guys want some dessert?

✰ Do you care for some dessert now?

4. I can ensure you that you will be impressed by our cheesecake and fall in love with it!

這樣我可以跟你保證你會被我們的起司蛋糕深深打動並愛上它。

✰ I guarantee that you will be touched by our cheesecake and fall in love with it.

✰ I truly believe that our cheesecake is the best in town and you will love it.

Unit 05

Serving Drinks
飲料服務

5.1 Ordering cocktail and champagne. 點調酒及香檳

 Dialogue 停不住對話

W ▶ Waiter 服務生 **P** ▶ Peter 彼得 **V** ▶ Vicky 薇琪

W ▶ Good evening, sir. Welcome to Red Roof Restaurant. How may I help you?

服務生 ▶ 先生，晚安。歡迎來到紅屋餐廳。有什麼能為您服務的嗎？

P ▶ Yes, please. I would like a table for two.

彼得 ▶ 是的。我想要兩人的位子。

W ▶ No problem, sir. This way, please.

服務生 ▶ 沒問題。請跟我來。

P ▶ Thank you.

彼得 ▶ 謝謝。

W ▸ Would you like to start with a cocktail?

服務生 ▸ 您想要先來杯雞尾酒嗎？

P ▸ Can you recommend something good?

彼得 ▸ 你可以建議不錯的嗎？

W ▸ How about a Screwdriver? It consists of vodka and orange juice.

服務生 ▸「螺絲起子」如何？它是伏特加和柳橙汁調製而成。

P ▸ Vodka and orange juice… sounds good. I will have a Screwdriver, please.

彼得 ▸ 伏特加和柳橙汁……聽起來不錯。我就來一杯「螺絲起子」。

W ▸ Sure, a Screwdriver for the gentleman. How about you, ma'am?

服務生 ▸ 沒問題。一杯「螺絲起子」給先生。小姐您呢？

V ▸ I am not a big fan of cocktail. I would rather order some wine with my meal.

薇琪 ▸ 我不是很喜歡雞尾酒。我比較想點葡萄酒來搭配我的餐點。

W ▸ Certainly. How about a bottle of champagne for you?

服務生 ▸ 沒問題，那來一瓶香檳如何？

V ▸ Terrific. I will take it.

薇琪 ▸ 很好，我就點香檳。

W ▸ We have Taittinger and Laurent Perrier to choose from. Which one would you prefer?

服務生 ▸ 我們有「泰廷爵」香檳和「法國羅蘭」香檳可供選擇。你想要哪一個？

01 Unit

02 Unit

03 Unit

04 Unit

05 Unit

06 Unit

07 Unit

08 Unit

V ▸ Is the Taittinger extra dry?

薇琪 ▸ 請問「泰廷爵」香檳甜度是略甜嗎？

W▸ Yes, it is. And I have to say it's very pleasant with red meat.

服務生 ▸ 是的。而且我必須說它搭配紅肉飲用非常棒。

V ▸ Really? Then I am going to try the T-bone Steak tonight.

薇琪 ▸ 真的嗎？那我今晚想試看看你們的丁骨牛排。

W▸ Perfect match! <u>I bet you will enjoy your dinner very much.</u>

服務生 ▸ 完美的搭配。我打賭您一定會非常喜歡您的晚餐。

P ▸ Excuse me. I am also thinking of ordering a glass of wine with my meal.

彼得 ▸ 不好意思。我也想點一杯葡萄酒來搭配主餐。

W▸ Sure. Do you have something particular in mind?

服務生 ▸ 沒問題。請問您心裡有特別想喝的嗎？

P ▸ I like white wine more.

彼得 ▸ 我比較喜歡白酒。

W▸ <u>May I ask what kind of white wine you would like, dry or sweet?</u>

服務生 ▸ 可以請問您喜歡哪一種白酒嗎？比較不甜還是比較甜的？

P ▸ Dry, I think.

彼得 ▸ 比較不甜的，我想。

W ▶ Then I will recommend Riesling 1981. It has well-balanced acidity and is very dry.

服務生 ▶ 那我會推薦1981年份的「麗斯琳」。它的酸度剛好且比較不甜。

P ▶ It sounds like what I want. One glass for me, please.

彼得 ▶ 聽起來像是我想要的。幫我點一杯，謝謝。

 Vocabulary 字彙

1. **cocktail** [`kɑkˌtel] **n** 名詞　雞尾酒
   On arrival, guests are offered wine or a champagne cocktail.
   每個賓客一到場都會有人送上紅酒或香檳雞尾酒。

2. **consist** [kən`sɪst] **v** 動詞　構成 [（+of）]
   We offer a healthy diet consisting of whole food.
   我們提供以天然食物構成的健康飲食。

3. **bottle** [`bɑt!] **n** 名詞　瓶子
   We had a nice meal with a bottle of champagne.
   我們美餐了一頓，還喝了一瓶香檳。。

4. **champagne** [ʃæm`pen] **n** 名詞　香檳酒
   Sorry, we don't have champagne today, but we do have a selection of sparkling wine for you to choose.
   很抱歉，我們今天沒有提供香檳，但我們有不同的氣泡酒可供選擇。

01 Unit
02 Unit
03 Unit
04 Unit
05 Unit
06 Unit
07 Unit
08 Unit

5. **match** [mætʃ] **n** 名詞　相配
This homemade bread is a perfect match for our chowder.
這個自製麵包很搭我們的海鮮濃湯。

6. **particular** [pɚˋtɪkjələ]　**adj** 形容詞　特別的；特定的
We are able to design a banquet menu to suit our guests'
particular needs.
我們可以設計一個宴會菜單來滿足賓客的特殊需求。

7. **well-balanced** [ˋwɛlˋbælənst]　**adj** 形容詞　勻稱的
The wine is full and dry with well - balanced acid.
此款酒干醇,很好的平衡了酸度.

8. **acidity** [əˋsɪdətɪ]　**n** 名詞　酸度
You can add some honey to counterbalance the acidity.
您可以加些蜂蜜來調和酸味。

In Other Words 這樣說也能通

1. It consists of vodka and orange juice.

它是伏特加和柳橙汁調製而成。

　⭐ It's made of vodka and orange juice.
　⭐ We use vodka and orange juice to make this.

2. I am not a big fan of cocktail. I would rather order some wine with my meal.

我不是很喜歡雞尾酒。我比較想點葡萄酒來搭配我的餐點。

　⭐ I don't really like cocktail, but I would like to order some wine with my meal.
　⭐ I am not ordering cocktail. Instead, I will order some with to go with my meal.

3. I bet you will enjoy your dinner very much.

我打賭您一定會非常喜歡您的晚餐。

　⭐ You will definitely enjoy your dinner very much.
　⭐ Trust me, your will enjoy your dinner a lot.

4. May I ask what kind of white wine you would like, dry or sweet?

可以請問您喜歡哪一種白酒嗎？比較不甜還是比較甜的？

　⭐ What kind of white wine do you prefer, dry or sweet?
　⭐ Would you please tell me that you like dry wine or sweet wine more?

01 Unit
02 Unit
03 Unit
04 Unit
05 Unit
06 Unit
07 Unit
08 Unit

Unit 05

Serving Drinks
飲料服務

5.2 **Welcome to Cheers Bar.** 歡迎來到Cheers酒吧

 Dialogue 停不住對話

B ▶ Bartender 調酒師   **G1 ▶ Mr.Roosevelt** 羅斯福先生
G2 ▶ Mrs. Roosevelt 羅斯福太太

B ▶ Welcome to Cheers Bar. Good afternoon, madam. Good afternoon, sir. What drinks would you like to have today?

調酒師 ▶ 歡迎來到Cheers酒吧。午安，女士。午安，先生。您們今天想點什麼飲料？

G1 ▶ I would like to try your martini, which I heard it's very good.

羅斯福先生 ▶ 我想試你們的「馬丁尼」，我聽說非常棒。

B ▸ Yes, it's a favorite among our regulars. Madam, how about you? A glass of martini for you as well?

調酒師 ▸ 是的，它是我們常客的最愛。您呢？女士。您也要來一杯「馬丁尼」嗎？

G2 ▸ I guess I will just have a bottle of Budweiser, please, and with a bucket of ice cubes.

羅斯福太太 ▸ 我想我來一瓶百威啤酒就好，和一桶冰塊。

B ▸ No problem. By the way, <u>what type of garnish would you like, sir? A cocktail onion, green olive, or lemon twist?</u>

調酒師 ▸ 沒問題。對了，先生，您想要哪一種裝飾物？珍珠洋蔥，綠橄欖，還是長條狀檸檬皮？

G1 ▸ I'd prefer a green olive, andI want my drink very dry.

羅斯福先生 ▸ 我想要綠橄欖，我想要辛辣口感的馬丁尼。

B ▸ Yes, I will make you a very dry martini. <u>Please allow me a couple of minutes to prepare your drink.</u>

調酒師 ▸ 好的，我會幫您調一杯口感辛辣的馬丁尼。請容許我花幾分鐘來調配您的飲料。

- -

B ▸ Here you are. A glass of martini for the gentleman and a bottle of Budweiser for the lady.

調酒師 ▸ 您的飲料。一杯馬丁尼給先生，和一瓶百威啤酒給小姐。

G2 ▸ Thank you.

羅斯福太太 ▸ 謝謝您。

B ▶ Here is your bill. It's US$25.

調酒師 ▶ 這是您的帳單。總金額是美金25元。

G2 ▶ Excuse me, may I also order one Roast Beef Roll to go with my beer?

羅斯福太太 ▶ 不好意思，我還可以點一份烤牛肉捲來搭配我的啤酒？

B ▶ Certainly. Sir, would you also like a roast beef roll? They are quite popular among our guests.

調酒師 ▶ 沒問題。 先生，您也要一些烤牛肉捲嗎？它蠻受我們客人歡迎的。

G1 ▶ No, thanks. I think I would like the Buffalo Wings more. I love spicy food!

羅斯福先生 ▶ 不了，謝謝。我想我比較喜歡辣雞翅。我喜歡吃辣！

B ▶ <u>Our Buffalo wings won't let you down. Trust me!</u> Then the total comes to US$35. Would you like to pay by cash or credit card?

調酒師 ▶ 我們的辣雞翅不會讓您失望。相信我！這樣總價是美金35元。您要用現金還是信用卡付帳？

G1 ▶ Neither of them. Would you please charge that to Room 2561?

羅斯福先生 ▶ 都不是。你可以把帳記到2561房嗎？

B ▶ Definitely. Thank you, sir.

調酒師 ▶ 當然，謝謝，先生。

Vocabulary 字彙

1. **favorite** [`fevərɪt] **n** 名詞 / **adj** 形容詞 特別喜愛的人（或物）；特別喜愛的

   Pepper is one of our chef's favorite spices.

   胡椒粉是我們主廚喜歡的一種調味品。

2. **bucket** [`bʌkɪt] **n** 名詞 水桶，提桶，吊桶

   Please bring five old fashion glasses and a bucket of ice to Table 8.

   請拿5個古典酒杯及一桶冰塊到第8桌。

3. **ice cube** [aɪs] [kjub] **n** 名詞 冰塊

   Please get me some ice cubes out of the fridge.

   請幫我從冰箱拿一些冰塊出來。

4. **garnish** [`gɑrnɪʃ] **n** 名詞 為增加色香味而添加的配菜；裝飾物

   The turkey was served with a garnish of parsley.

   做好的火雞上面配上歐芹作點綴。

5. **olive** [`ɑlɪv] **n** 名詞 橄欖

   The chef asked me to combine the beans, chopped mint, and olive oil in a large bowl.

   主廚要我把菜豆、切碎的薄荷和橄欖油放在大碗裡攪拌。

6. **bill** [bɪl] **n** 名詞 帳單

   Did the guests at Table 11 sign the bill yet?

   11桌的客人簽帳單了嗎？

7.**spicy** [`spaɪsɪ]　adj 形容詞　辛辣的

In my opinions, the spicy flavors in these dishes call for reds rather than whites.

我認為這些菜的味道辛辣應該搭配紅酒而不是白酒。

8.**charge** [tʃɑrdʒ]　v 動詞　索價；對……索費

Most restaurants in the country charge 10% service fee in lieu of tipping.

這個國家大部分的餐廳收10%服務費以取代小費。

In Other Words 這樣說也能通

01
Unit

02
Unit

03
Unit

04
Unit

05
Unit

06
Unit

07
Unit

08
Unit

1. I would like to try your martini, which I heard it's very good.

我想試你們的「馬丁尼」，我聽說非常棒。

★ I am told that your martini is very good and therefore I would like to try it.

★ It seems that your martini is very popular and I would like to order it.

2. What type of garnish would you like, sir? A cocktail onion, green olive, or lemon twist?

先生想要哪一種裝飾物？珍珠洋蔥，綠橄欖，還是長條狀檸檬皮？

★ We offer three garnish selections: a cocktail onion, green olive, and lemon twist. Which one would you prefer, sir?

★ As for the garnish, what would you like? A cocktail onion, green olive, or lemon twist?

3. Please allow me a couple of minutes to prepare your drink.

請容許我花幾分鐘來調配您的飲料。

★ It takes me couple minutes to prepare your drink. Please wait.

★ Your drink will be ready in a couple of minutes. Please wait.

4. Our Buffalo wings won't let you down. Trust me!

我們的辣雞翅不曾讓您失望。相信我！

★ I am proud of our Buffalo wings, and you will like it.

★ I bet you will like our Buffalo wings very much.

Unit 05

Serving Drinks
飲料服務

5.3

I don't feel like drinking anything with alcohol now. 我現在不想喝含酒精的飲料

 Dialogue 停不住對話

W ▶ Waitress 服務生　**G1** ▶ Guest 1 客人1
G2 ▶ Guest 2 客人2

W ▶ This is our menu, sir. Take your time. Would you prefer an aperitif while you're looking over the menu?

服務生 ▶ 先生，這是我們的菜單。請慢慢看。您在看菜單的同時會想要來一杯雞尾酒嗎？

G1 ▶ An aperitif? Probably not. I do feel thirsty, but I don't feel like drinking anything with alcohol now.

客人1 ▶ 雞尾酒？大概不用了。我是覺得渴，但我現在不想喝含酒精的飲料。

118

W ▶ I see. Then I will recommend our non-alcoholic fruit cocktails. <u>We have a list of non-alcoholic fruit cocktails here on the second page of our drink list.</u> Maybe you would like to try our Banana Colada. It's made with banana, milk, pineapple juice, coconut cream and sugar. It's very refreshing and I believe you will like it. And today, it's only half price.

G1 ▶ Sounds nice. How about the Princess Margaret? Could you tell me what that is?

W ▶ Princess Margaret? <u>I would say fruit lovers will absolutely die for a Princess Margaret.</u> It's made of strawberries, pineapple slices, orange juice, and lemon juice. <u>This beautiful fruit cocktail beverage will look particularly attractive served with a red straw and a fresh strawberry on the rim of the glass.</u>

G1 ▶ The mix of fruits really attracts me. I will take a Princess Margaret.

服務生 ▶ 了解。那我會推薦我們非酒精性的水果雞尾酒。在我們飲料單上的第二頁有列出所有的非酒精性水果雞尾酒。或許你會喜歡我們的香蕉可樂達。我們用香蕉、牛奶、鳳梨汁、椰子奶油和糖做的。它非常提神，我相信您會喜歡。而且今天只要半價。

客人1 ▶ 聽起來很棒。那「瑪格麗特公主」呢？你可以告訴我那是什麼嗎？

服務生 ▶ 「瑪格麗特公主」嗎？我會説水果愛好者一定會很喜歡「瑪格麗特公主」。它是用草莓、鳳梨片、柳橙汁和檸檬汁做成的。搭配上紅色吸管和杯緣的新鮮草莓，這一杯美麗的水果雞尾酒飲料會看起來特別吸引人。

客人1 ▶ 綜合水果很吸引我。我就點「瑪格麗特公主」。

01 Unit
02 Unit
03 Unit
04 Unit
05 Unit
06 Unit
07 Unit
08 Unit

W ▶ How about you, sir?

服務生 ▶ 先生您呢？

G2 ▶ I would like to have an aperitif. What types of aperitifs do you offer?

客人2 ▶ 我想點開胃酒。你們有什麼種類的開胃酒？

W ▶ We have Campari and Aperol.

服務生 ▶ 我們有「康柏力」酒和「阿佩羅」酒。

G2 ▶ I have no idea what they are. I will be grateful if you can explain more.

客人2 ▶ 我完全不知道那是什麼。我會很謝謝你如果你能解釋多一點。

W ▶ My pleasure. Campari is an Italian aperitif with distinctively bitter, herbal, slightly spicy, and grapefruit taste. Aperol is a bright orange-hued drink with a pleasant flavor.

服務生 ▶ 我的榮幸。「康柏力」是一種義大利開胃酒，它有很特殊的苦味，草本的，微辣的葡萄柚口味。「阿佩羅」有明亮的柳橙顏色和令人愉悅的口感。

G2 ▶ I will go for a Campari.

客人2 ▶ 那我點「康柏力」。

W ▶ Thank you, sir.

服務生 ▶ 先生謝謝您。

Vocabulary 字彙

01 Unit

02 Unit

03 Unit

04 Unit

05 Unit

06 Unit

07 Unit

08 Unit

1. **aperitif** [ɑperiˋtif] **n** 名詞　開胃酒
No, thanks. We will skip the aperitif.
不用了，謝謝。飯前酒就免了。

2. **thirsty** [ˋθɝstɪ] **adj** 形容詞　口乾的，渴的
I am so thirsty. Would you please bring me a glass of water first?
我好渴，可以先給我一杯開水嗎？

3. **alcoholic** [͵ælkəˋhɔlɪk] **adj** 形容詞　含酒精的
The alcoholic strength of brandy far exceeds that of wine.
白蘭地的酒精濃度遠遠超過葡萄酒。

4. **refreshing** [rɪˋfrɛʃɪŋ] **adj** 形容詞　提神的；清涼的
This is a refreshing and energizing fruit drink.
這是一個提神且能增進體力的果汁飲料。

5. **beverage** [kwɪˋzin] **n** 名詞　飲料
We provide complete food & beverage service for company meetings.
我們為您的公司會議提供全方位的餐飲服務。

6. **straw** [strɔ] **n** 名詞　吸管
May I have a straw for my drink?
給我一個喝飲料的吸管好嗎？

7. herbal [`hɝb!]　adj 形容詞　草本的

We can guarantee that our range of herbal teas contain no preservatives, colorings or artificial flavorings.

我們可以保證我們一系列的花草茶不含防腐劑、色素和人工香料。

8. flavor [`flevɚ]　n 名詞　味道

Fry quickly to seal in the flavor of the meat.

快速煎一下以鎖住肉的美味。

 In Other Words 這樣說也能通

1. I do feel thirsty, but I don't feel like drinking anything with alcohol now.

我是覺得渴，但我現在不想喝含酒精的飲料。

☆ I am really thirsty, but I don't want to order any alcoholic drink now.

☆ I am indeed thirsty, but I don't want to drink alcohol now.

2. We have a list of nonalcoholic fruit cocktails here on the second page of our drink list.

在我們飲料單上的第二頁有列出所有的非酒精性水果雞尾酒。

☆ A selection of nonalcoholic fruit cocktails is listed on the second page of our drink list.

☆ You can see all our nonalcoholic fruit cocktails on the second page of our drink list.

3. I would say fruit lovers will absolutely die for a Princess Margaret.

我會說水果愛好者一定會很喜歡「瑪格麗特公主」。

⭐ I would say the Princess Margaret will attract many fruit lovers.

⭐ People who like fruits will absolutely enjoy our Princess Margaret.

4. This beautiful fruit cocktail beverage will look particularly attractive served with a red straw and a fresh strawberry on the rim of the glass.

這個美麗的水果雞尾酒飲料會看起來特別吸引人，配有紅色吸管和新鮮草莓在杯緣。

⭐ We serve this beautiful fruit cocktail beverage in a particular attractive way with a red straw and a fresh strawberry on the rim of the glass.

⭐ This beautiful fruit cocktail beverage has a red straw and a fresh strawberry on the rim of the glass, and therefore looks very attractive.

01 Unit
02 Unit
03 Unit
04 Unit
05 Unit
06 Unit
07 Unit
08 Unit

Unit 05

Serving Drinks
飲料服務

5.4

Would you like some wine with your meal? 您想要點葡萄酒搭配您的餐點嗎

 Dialogue 停不住對話

W ▶ Waiter 服務生　**G1** ▶ Guest 1　客人1
G2 ▶ Guest 2 客人2

W ▶ Miss, let me repeat your order. You've ordered the oyster as appetizer and sirloin steak as the main dish.

服務生 ▶ 小姐，讓我重複您點的餐，您點了生蠔作為開胃菜，主菜是沙朗牛排。

G1 ▶ That's correct. Thank you.

客人1 ▶ 正確，謝謝您。

W ▶ Would you like some wine with your meal?

服務生 ▶ 您想要點葡萄酒搭配您的餐點嗎？

G1 ▸ Why not? May I take a look of your wine list?

客人1 ▸好啊。可以看一下你們的酒單嗎？

W ▸ Sure. Here you are.

服務生 ▸當然。在這裡。

The waiter passed the wine list to the guest.

服務生把酒單地給客人。

G1 ▸ You certainly have a very extensive cellar, and I have no clue what I should order.

客人1 ▸您店裡的酒種類真的好多，且我完全不知道該點什麼。

W ▸ I would recommend Chablis, which is white wine and I think it will go very well with the oyster.

服務生 ▸我會推薦「夏布利」。它是一種白酒，而且非常搭配您點的生蠔。

G1 ▸ But the price is over my budget. Do you sell it by the glass?

客人1 ▸但價格超出我的預算。你們可以以杯計價嗎？

W ▸ I am afraid we don't, but you can order a half-bottle. The price is quite attractive.

服務生 ▸很遺憾我們沒辦法這樣賣，但您可以點小瓶的。價格還蠻實惠的

G1 ▸ Well… okay. It would fall within my price range.

客人1 ▸好吧，這還算符合我的預算。

W ▸ So, a half-bottle of Chablis for you, miss.

服務生 ▸所以幫您點小瓶的「夏布利」酒。

01 Unit
02 Unit
03 Unit
04 Unit
05 Unit
06 Unit
07 Unit
08 Unit

G1 ▶ Yes, please.

客人1 ▶ 是的，請。

W ▶ <u>Sir, the set menu that you ordered includes a complimentary glass of wine to go with your main dish.</u> Would you like to try our house red for your steak?

服務生 ▶ 先生，您點的套餐可以點一杯酒搭配主餐。您想試試我們的招牌紅酒配您的牛排嗎？

G2 ▶ House red? What kind of wine is that?

客人2 ▶ 招牌紅酒？這是什麼酒？

W ▶ It's the wine recommended by our chef.

服務生 ▶ 是我們主廚推薦的紅酒。

G2 ▶ What does it taste like?

客人2 ▶ 嚐起來如何？

W ▶ If you prefer a light wine, you will enjoy it.

服務生 ▶ 如果你偏好清淡的酒，你會喜歡它。

G2 ▶ No, <u>I would rather have a good, dry, full-bodied red wine.</u>

客人2 ▶ 不，我寧願要一個好的，較不甜，且醇厚的紅酒。

W ▶ Then I think the Mouton will meet your expectation.

服務生 ▶ 那我想「摩當」酒會符合您的期待。

G2 ▶ OK, I will just follow your advice. One glass of Mouton, please.

客人2 ▶ 就聽您的建議。請給我一杯「摩當」酒。

W ▶ Will that be all?

服務生 ▶ 還有其他要點的嗎？

G2 ▶ Yes.

客人**2** ▶沒有了。

W ▶ The piano play will begin soon, and I will be right back with your appetizers.

服務生 ▶鋼琴演奏馬上就要開始了。我會立即上您們的開胃菜。

 Vocabulary 字彙

1. **oyster** [ˋɔɪstɚ] **n** 名詞　蠔、牡蠣
   I can offer you some oyster soup, compliments of our chef.
   我可以免費提供你牡蠣湯，是我們主廚的一點敬意。

2. **appetizer** [ˋæpəˏtaɪzɚ] **n** 名詞　開胃菜
   We'll serve some crackers and cheese as an appetizer. I hope you will like it.
   我們將會上一些餅乾和奶酪作為開胃品，希望您喜歡。

3. **extensive** [ɪkˋstɛnsɪv] **adj** 形容詞　廣泛的
   This chain restaurant lay in extensive stores of food supplies.
   這個連鎖餐廳儲存大量食物。

4. **cellar** [ˋsɛlɚ] **n** 名詞　酒窖
   Please help yourselves to the wine in the cellar.
   酒窖裡的酒都可隨您飲用。

5. **recommend** [ˏrɛkəˋmɛnd] **v** 動詞　推薦，建議
   I recommend that you avoid processed foods whenever possible.
   我建議你儘可能避免加工食品。

6. **budget** [ˋbʌdʒɪt]   n 名詞   預算
Offering budget-priced meals doesn't necessary mean compromising on food quality.
提供機濟實惠的餐點不一定就表示犧牲食物的品質。

7. **chef** [ʃɛf]   n 名詞   主廚
The chef is pleased to cater for vegetarian diets.
主廚很樂意為客人製作素食餐點。

8. **taste** [test]   v 動詞   吃起來；嚐起來
You can salt the stock to your taste and leave it simmering very gently.
你可以依據你自己的口味給湯底加點鹽，然後用小火慢燉。

In Other Words 這樣說也能通

1. You certainly have a very extensive cellar, and I have no clue what I should order.
   您店裡的酒種類真的好多，且我完全不知道該點什麼。
   ⭐ You have such a wide selection of wine that I have no idea what to order.
   ⭐ The extensive cellar you have makes it hard for me to make a selection.

2. But the price is over my budget.
   但價格超出我的預算。
   ⭐ But this is not something I can afford.
   ⭐ The price is too high for me.

3. Sir, the set menu that you ordered includes a complimentary glass of wine to go with your main dish.
   先生，您點的套餐可以點一杯酒搭配主餐。
   ⭐ Sir, since you ordered the set menu, you can claima glass of wine for free to go with your main dish.
   ⭐ You can order a glass of wine to go with your main dish, and it's included in the set menu.

4. I would rather have a good, dry, full-bodied red wine.
   我寧願要一個好的，較不甜，且醇厚的紅酒。
   ⭐ I would prefer a good, fry, full-bodied red wine.
   ⭐ I would rather have a glass of red wine that is good, dry, and full-bodied.

01 Unit
02 Unit
03 Unit
04 Unit
05 Unit
06 Unit
07 Unit
08 Unit

Unit 06
Serving During a Meal
餐間服務

6.1 ## Are you ready for your main dishes? 可以上主餐了嗎

 Dialogue 停不住對話　　🎧21

W ▶ Waiter 服務生　　**G1** ▶ Guest 1 (the husband) 客人1（先生）
G2 ▶ Guest 2 (the wife) 客人2（太太）
G3 ▶ Guest 3 (the son) 客人3（兒子）
G4 ▶ Guest 4 (the daughter) 客人4（女兒）

W ▶ <u>Are you done with your appetizers?</u> May I take the dishes away?

服務生 ▶ 您的開胃菜用完了嗎？可以收您的盤子了嗎？

G1 ▶ My wife and I are done with it. Please leave my son and daughter's plates.

客人1 ▶ 我太太和我用完了。我兒子和女兒的盤子請待會收。

W ▸ Sure, no problem! I will just take your plates for now. Are you ready for your main dishes?

服務生 ▸ 當然，沒問題！現在先收您們兩位的盤子。可以上您們的主菜了嗎？

G1 ▸ Yes, please. You can serve all the four dishes together.

客人1 ▸ 好的，請。你可以把所有主菜一起上。

W ▸ Yes, sir.

服務生 ▸ 好的。

Ten minutes later　十分鐘後

W ▸ The medium Sirloin Steak is for the gentleman, and the medium-well T-bone Steak is for you, ma'am. Be careful. The plates are very hot.

服務生 ▸ 這是先生點的沙朗牛排，五分熟。這是女士您點的丁骨牛排，八分熟。小心，盤子很燙。

G1 ▸ Yes, thank you.

客人1 ▸ 是的，謝謝您。

G2 ▸ Oh, wow! The steaks look juicy and mouthwatering.

客人2 ▸ 哇！這牛排看起來好多汁，讓人口水直流。

W ▸ Thank you. I am proud to say that we have the best steaks in town. And this is the beef burger with onion rings for the little gentleman. We have ketchup and mustard for the

服務生 ▸ 謝謝您。我很驕傲地說我們的牛排是城裡最好的。這是小帥哥點的牛肉漢堡和洋蔥圈。洋蔥圈可以搭配番

<u>onion rings.</u> Which one do you prefer?

茄醬或芥末醬，你比較喜歡哪一個？

G3 ▶ May I have both?

客人3 ▶ 我可以兩個都要嗎？

W ▶ Why not? Here you are! And the Seafood Pasta for the lady.

服務生 ▶ 當然可以！這是您的番茄醬和芥末醬。最後是小姐的海鮮義大利麵。

G4 ▶ Thank you. May I have some hot sauce for my pasta, please?

客人4 ▶ 謝謝你。請問可以給我一些辣椒醬搭配義大利麵吃嗎？

W ▶ We only have TABASCO. Is that ok with you?

服務生 ▶ 我們只有 TABASCO，可以嗎？

G4 ▶ Definitely, I love it.

客人4 ▶ 當然，我很喜歡TABASCO。

W ▶ Please enjoy your dinner. Is there anything else I can help you with?

服務生 ▶ 請享用您們的晚餐。還有什麼可以為您服務的嗎？

G1 ▶ <u>I wonder if we can have another basket of your freshly baked bread.</u> <u>The bread is so yummy that we all enjoyed it so much!</u>

客人1 ▶ 我們可以再來一籃你們新鮮烘焙的麵包嗎？你們的麵包真好吃，我們都很喜歡。

W ▶ No problem. I will be right back with your bread.

服務生 ▶ 沒問題。我馬上拿一籃來。

Vocabulary 字彙

1. **serve** [sɝv] **v** 動詞　侍候（顧客等）；供應（飯菜）；端上
I will top the fish with the cooked leeks before I serve it.
在端上桌之前我會把炒好的韭蔥覆蓋在魚上。

2. **juicy** [ˋdʒusɪ] **adj** 形容詞　多汁的
You can use the knife to slip through the outer part and you will see the meat inside is very tender and juicy.
你可以用刀把表面劃開，然後你會看到裡面的肉非常軟嫩多汁。

3. **mouthwatering** [mɑʊθ ˋwɔtərɪŋ] **adj** 形容詞　令人垂涎的
Many of our guests said this tender beef dish is mouthwatering.
我們很多客人都說這道嫩牛肉令人垂涎三尺。

4. **burger** [ˋbɝgɚ] **n** 名詞　漢堡
We add mushrooms, red peppers, and onions to our cheeseburger.
我們的起司漢堡加了蘑菇、紅椒、和洋蔥。

5. **pasta** [ˋpɑstə] **n** 名詞　義大利麵
Would you please share the pasta out between two plates?
你可以將義大利麵平分到兩個盤子裡嗎？

6. **sauce** [sɔs] **n** 名詞　調味醬，醬汁
I recommend you pour a little of the sauce over the chicken.
我建議你在雞肉上淋一些醬汁。

01 Unit
02 Unit
03 Unit
04 Unit
05 Unit
06 Unit
07 Unit
08 Unit

7. **bread** [brɛd] **n** 名詞 麵包

Have you got any cheese I can have with this bread?

你有沒有起司我可以夾麵包吃？

8. **yummy** [ˋjʌmɪ] **adj** 形容詞 好吃的；美味的

Just thinking of all that yummy food makes my mouth water.

光想到那些美味的食物就讓我口水直流。

In Other Words 這樣說也能通

1. Are you done with your appetizers?

您的開胃菜用完了嗎？

⭐ Have you finished your appetizers?

⭐ Are you still eating your appetizers?

2. We have ketchup and mustard for the onion rings.

洋蔥圈可以搭配番茄醬或芥末醬。

⭐ You can have either ketchup or mustard for the onion rings.

⭐ We offer ketchup and mustard for you to go with the onion rings.

3. I wonder if we can have another basket of your freshly baked bread.

我們可以再來一籃你們新鮮烘焙的麵包嗎？

⭐ May I have some more of your freshly baked bread?

⭐ Would you please give us another basket of your freshly baked bread?

4. The bread is so yummy that we all enjoyed it so much!

你們的麵包真好吃，我們都很喜歡。

⭐ The bread is very tasty and we all like it very much!

⭐ The bread tastes so good that we all enjoyed it very much!

Unit 06

Serving During a Meal
餐間服務

6.2

Would you tell me where the lady's room is? 可以告訴我女用化妝間在哪

 Dialogue 停不住對話   22

W ▶ Waitress 服務生   G1 ▶ Guest 1 客人1
G2 ▶ Guest 2 客人2

W ▶ Excuse me. Your pumpkin soup, ma'am. And this is your French onion soup, sir. Please enjoy your soups. I recommend you eat the bread with the soup. They are the perfect match!

服務生 ▶ 不好意思。女士，這是您的南瓜湯。先生，這是您的法式洋蔥湯。請享用您的湯品。我建議搭配麵包一起吃。麵包和湯很搭。

G1 ▶ Thanks for your advice. We will try it.

客人1 ▶ 謝謝您的建議。我們會試試看。

01
Unit

W ▶ May I take away your soup bowl, sir?

服務生 ▶ 先生，可以收您的湯碗了嗎？

G1 ▶ Sure, go ahead.

客人1 ▶ 當然，請。

02
Unit

G2 ▶ I can't finish it. You can also take away mine.

客人2 ▶ 我喝不完，你也可以把我的收走。

W ▶ Yes, ma'am. I will be right back with your entrées.

服務生 ▶ 好的，女士。我會馬上上您們的主餐。

03
Unit

W ▶ Thank you for waiting. This is your Roasted Lamb Chops, ma'am, and this is the Pan-fried Salmon Fish Fillet for you, sir.

服務生 ▶ 謝謝您的等待。女士，這是您的烤羊排。先生，這是您的乾煎鮭魚排。

04
Unit

G1&G2 ▶ Thank you.

客人1&客人2 ▶ 謝謝。

05
Unit

W ▶ <u>The side dish to go with the roasted lamb chops is mashed potatoes</u>, and we serve the fish fillet with French fries.

服務生 ▶ 烤羊排的配菜是薯泥。乾煎鮭魚排的配菜是炸薯條。

06
Unit

G2 ▶ They look so tasty!

客人2 ▶ 看起來真美味。

07
Unit

W ▶ Please enjoy your meals.

服務生 ▶ 請享用您的餐點。

08
Unit

W ▶ May I clear the table for you?

服務生 ▶ 可以幫您清空桌子了嗎？

G1 ▶ Yes, please.

客人1 ▶ 好的，請。

W ▶ How do you feel about the meals that we served? Did you enjoy it?

服務生 ▶ 覺得我們的餐點如何？喜歡嗎？

G2 ▶ Your salmon fillet is very tender and juicy. I like it very much.

客人2 ▶ 你們的鮭魚排軟嫩又多汁，我非常喜歡。

G1 ▶ I have to say that the chef overcooked the lamb chops. The meat was too tough. But I like your mashed potatoes very much.

客人1 ▶ 我必須說你們的烤羊排煮過頭了。肉吃起來有點老。但我非常喜歡你們的薯泥。

W ▶ I am sorry to hear that. I will tell our chef what you said. Are you ready for your desserts?

服務生 ▶ 很抱歉。我會轉告我們主廚。可以上甜點了嗎？

G1 ▶ Why not?

客人1 ▶ 為何不？

W ▶ Your Banana Split Sundae and Tiramisu. Please enjoy!

服務生 ▶ 您們的香蕉船聖代和提拉米蘇。請享用。

G2 ▶ Thank you, sir. By the way, would you tell me where the lady's room is?

客人2 ▶ 先生，謝謝您。對了，可以告訴我你們的女用化妝間在哪嗎？

W ▶ Certainly, madam. The lady's room is on the second floor. Go upstairs and you will see it on your left hand side.

服務生 ▶ 當然。我們的女用化妝間在二樓。上樓後在你的左手邊。

01 Unit
02 Unit
03 Unit
04 Unit
05 Unit
06 Unit
07 Unit
08 Unit

Vocabulary 字彙

1. **bowl** [bol] n 名詞　碗
The guest finished off two bowls of noodles in no time.
這個客人很快就吃完兩碗麵。

2. **entrée** [`ɑntre] n 名詞　主菜
Our waiters will enquire if the guests are satisfied with the meals and services ten minutes after they receive their entrée.
在客人用主菜十分鐘後我們的服務生會詢問他們對餐點和服務是否滿意。

3. **roast** [rost] v 動詞　烤
The menu features roast beef, pork, and duck.
菜單上特色菜是烤牛肉、烤豬肉、和烤鴨。

4. **chop** [tʃɑp] n 名詞　（豬，羊的）肋骨肉，排骨
The chef seasons the pork chop before frying it.
主廚在煎豬排前會先調味。

5. **fillet** [`fɪlɪt] n 名詞　里脊肉（片）；魚片
We offer all kinds of specific roasted eel, prawn, and fillet.
我們提供各式各樣高品質的烤曼魚，大蝦，和魚片。

6.**mash** [mæʃ] **v** 動詞　把……搗成糊狀
Will mashed potatoes be all right for both of you?
兩位都點薯泥嗎？

7.**tender** [`tɛndɚ] **adj** 形容詞　嫩的；柔軟的
We cook the meat slowly until it's tender.
我們把肉用慢火煮爛。

8.**sundae** [`sʌnde] **n** 名詞　聖代冰淇淋
Our strawberry sundae is on sale this week.
我們的草莓聖代這週特價。

In Other Words 這樣說也能通

1. The side dish to go with the roasted lamb chops is mashed potatoes.

   烤羊排的配菜是薯泥。

   ⭐ We serve the roasted lamb chops with mashed potatoes.

   ⭐ The side dish of the roasted lamb chops is mashed potatoes.

2. How do you feel about the meals we served?

   覺得我們的餐點如何？

   ⭐ How do you like your meals?

   ⭐ May I ask about your opinions on the meals we served?

3. Are you ready for your desserts?

   可以上甜點了嗎？

   ⭐ May I serve your desserts now?

   ⭐ Is it time for your desserts?

4. Would you tell me where the lady's room is?

   可以告訴我你們的女用化妝間在哪嗎？

   ⭐ May I ask where the lady's room is?

   ⭐ Excuse me, where is your lady's room?

01 Unit
02 Unit
03 Unit
04 Unit
05 Unit
06 Unit
07 Unit
08 Unit

Unit 06

Serving During a Meal
餐間服務

6.3

Do you have any sauce for my fried shrimps? 有任何沾醬可以搭配我的炸蝦嗎

 *Dialogue* 停不住對話

W ▶ Waitress 服務生　**G1** ▶ Guest 1　客人1
G2 ▶ Guest 2　客人2

G1 ▶ Excuse me.

客人1 ▶不好意思。

W ▶ Yes, how can I help you?

服務生 ▶是的，有什麼能為您服務的？

G1 ▶ <u>Could you please bring me another knife</u>? This knife is not sharp enough.

客人1 ▶可以再給我一個刀子嗎？這個刀子不夠利。

W ▶ No problem. Anything else?

服務生 ▶沒問題。還有別的嗎？

G2 ▶ Could you also refill my water? I am quite thirsty.

客人**2** ▶可以幫我把水倒滿嗎？我還蠻渴的。

W ▶ Sure, I will bring the knife and water right away.

服務生 ▶當然，立刻幫您把刀子和水拿來。

During the meal 用餐中

G1 ▶ Excuse me. The salt and pepper shakers are empty.

客人**1** ▶不好意思，鹽巴和胡椒罐是空的。

W ▶ Sorry about that. I will bring you other shakers.

服務生 ▶很抱歉，我現在幫您更換。

G2 ▶ Do you have any sauce for my fried shrimps?

客人**2** ▶你們有任何沾醬可以搭配我的炸蝦嗎？

W ▶ We have ketchup, mustard, chili sauce, and mayonnaise. Which one would you prefer?

服務生 ▶ 我們有番茄醬、芥末醬、辣椒醬、美乃滋。您喜歡哪一個？

G2 ▶ I'll have the chili sauce. I love spicy food.

客人**2** ▶我要辣椒醬。我喜歡吃辣。

W ▶ Got it. I will be right back.

服務生 ▶了解，馬上替您拿來。

After the meal 用餐後

W ▶ Do you care for some desserts?

服務生 ▶有想要來點甜點嗎？

01 Unit

02 Unit

03 Unit

04 Unit

05 Unit

06 Unit

07 Unit

08 Unit

G2 ▶ I do. May I have a Chocolate Soufflé?

客人2 ▶ 我要。我要點巧克力舒芙蕾。

W ▶ I'm not sure if we have any Chocolate Soufflé left. Please allow me to check.

服務生 ▶ 我不確定現在還有沒有巧克力舒芙蕾。請容許我去確認。

- -

W ▶ Sorry, madam. Now we only have Mango Cheese Cake and Fruit Tart. Would you like to try either of it?

服務生 ▶ 小姐，抱歉。我們現在只有芒果起司蛋糕和水果塔。想要試試嗎？

G2 ▶ That's too bad. I really like your Chocolate Soufflés.

客人2 ▶ 真糟糕。我非常喜歡你們的巧克力舒芙蕾。

W ▶ Our Mango Cheese Cake and Fruit Tart are also very delectable. <u>I bet you will like both of them.</u>

服務生 ▶ 芒果起司蛋糕和水果塔一樣很好吃。我打賭你兩個都會喜歡。

G2 ▶ OK, then I will try your Mango Cheese Cake.

客人2 ▶ 好吧，那我就試試你們的芒果起司蛋糕。

- -

W ▶ Should I bring your after-meal coffee?

服務生 ▶ 可以幫您們上餐後咖啡了嗎？

G1 ▶ Yes, please. I ordered an Espresso, and a Cappuccino for my friends.

客人1 ▶ 好的，請。我點的是espresso，我朋友是cappuccino。

01 Unit
02 Unit
03 Unit
04 Unit
05 Unit
06 Unit
07 Unit
08 Unit

W ▶ Yes. Regular or decaf?

服務生 ▶ 我知道。一般還是無咖啡因？

G1 ▶ Regular, please.

客人1 ▶ 請給我一般咖啡。

G2 ▶ Decaf, thank you. Would you also bring us some sugar, please?

客人2 ▶ 我要無咖啡因的，謝謝。可以給我們糖嗎？

W ▶ Certainly.

服務生 ▶ 當然。

 Vocabulary 字彙

1. **knife** [naɪf] **n** 名詞　刀，小刀；菜刀
Our pastry chef usually trims off the excess pastry using a sharp knife.
我們的點心師傅通常會用銳利的刀切去多餘的餅皮。

2. **salt** [sɔlt] **n** 名詞　鹽
Please salt the stock to your taste and leave it simmering very gently.
請依自己的口味給高湯加點鹽，然後用小火慢燉。

3. **pepper** shaker [ˋpɛpɚ ˋʃekɚ] **n** 名詞　胡椒鹽罐
Waiter, please bring me a pepper shaker. I can't find any on the table.
服務生，請給我胡椒鹽罐。桌上沒有。

4.**mayonnaise** [ˌmeə`nez] **n** 名詞　美乃滋
We use light or non-fat mayonnaise when making coleslaw and potato salad.
我們用低脂或脫脂美乃滋做涼拌捲心菜和馬鈴薯沙拉。

5.**chili** [`tʃɪlɪ] **n** 名詞　紅辣椒
Would you please add some more chili to the sauce? It's not spicy enough.
你可以在醬料裡加多一點辣椒嗎？還不夠辣。

6.**soufflé** [su`fle] **n** 名詞　舒芙蕾（以起泡蛋白為主烤成的酥鬆食品）
The soufflé is the best I have ever tasted.
這個舒芙蕾是我吃過最好吃的。

7.**cheese** [tʃiz] **vi** 名詞　乳酪
You can sprinkle cheese on egg or vegetable dishes.
你可以把奶酪撒在蛋或蔬菜做的菜餚上。

8.**tart** [tɑrt] **n** 名詞　水果塔
The tea goes with this lemon tart perfectly.
這個茶配上這檸檬塔非常完美。

In Other Words 這樣說也能通

1. **Could you please bring me another knife?**
   可以再給我一個刀子嗎？
   ✰ May I have another knife?
   ✰ Another knife, please. Thank you.

2. **Could you also refill my water?**
   可以幫我把水填滿嗎？
   ✰ May I have some more water?
   ✰ Would you please add some water for me?

3. **Do you have any sauce for my fried shrimps?**
   你們有任何沾醬可以搭配我的炸蝦嗎？
   ✰ I would like to have some dipping sauce for my Fried Shrimps, please.
   ✰ Do you have any sauce that goes with the fried shrimps well?

4. **I bet you will like both of them.**
   我打賭你兩個都會喜歡。
   ✰ I believe you will be satisfied with both of them.
   ✰ Trust me, both of them will not disappoint you.

Unit 06

Serving During a Meal
餐間服務

6.4

May I demonstrate the steps of eating the roast duck? 我可以為您示範吃烤鴨的步驟嗎

 Dialogue 停不住對話

W ▶ Waitress 服務生　**G** ▶ Guest 客人

W ▶ I'm sorry for having kept you waiting. Here is your appetizer. Please enjoy.

服務生 ▶ 抱歉讓您等待。這是您的開胃菜，請享用。

G ▶ Woo, it looks very delicate. What are the ingredients in it?

客人 ▶ 看起來好雅緻。裡面是什麼食材？

W ▶ The chef has put mixed seasonal vegetables and prawns in it. The prawns in this season are very sweet and tender.

服務生 ▶ 主廚放了多種當季蔬菜和明蝦。這季的明蝦很鮮甜軟嫩。

G ▸ That's great. I am a big fan of prawns.

客人 ▸ 太好了。我非常喜歡吃明蝦。

W ▸ May I serve the soup now?

服務生 ▸ 可以為您上湯了嗎？

G ▸ Yes, please.

客人 ▸ 好的，請。

W ▸ Be careful. It's very hot.

服務生 ▸ 小心，這很燙。

G ▸ Oh, thanks for your consideration.

客人 ▸ 謝謝您的關心。

W ▸ Here's the Beijing Roast Duck. May I demonstrate the steps of eating the roast duck?

服務生 ▸ 現在為您上北京烤鴨。我可以為您示範吃烤鴨的步驟嗎？

G ▸ Yes, please. <u>This is my first time to try Beijing Roast Duck.</u>

客人 ▸ 好的，請。這是我第一次嘗試北京烤鴨。

W ▸ First, take a piece of the sliced duck meat and dip it into the sweet bean paste. Then lay it on the steam pancake and add some spring onions. Finally, fold the wrapping around the filling and then you can enjoy it.

服務生 ▸ 首先，將鴨肉沾上甜麵醬，然後把鴨肉放在包裹的麵皮上，再加一些大蔥。最後把麵皮順著包裹的餡料折起來就可以吃了。

G ▸ Thank you very much for your

客人 ▸ 非常謝謝您的示

demonstration. I appreciate that. | 範。

G ▶ Excuse me. | 客人 ▶ 服務生，請過來一下。

W ▶ Yes, sir. What can I do for you? | 服務生 ▶ 好的，先生。需要我幫您什麼忙？

G ▶ I would like to have more spring onions and sweet bean paste. The duck tastes extremely flavorful with spring onions and sweet bean paste. | 客人 ▶ 我想要多一點甜麵醬和蔥。鴨肉和著甜麵醬和大蔥吃起來非常有風味。

W ▶ Good to hear that. I will bring you some more right away. | 服務生 ▶ 很高興聽到您這麼說。我馬上幫您拿一些過來。

G ▶ Excuse me. I've ordered an apple cider, but I changed my mind now. May I have a glass of lemonade? | 客人 ▶ 不好意思，我之前點了蘋果西打，現在我改變主意。可以點一杯檸檬水嗎？

W ▶ No problem. Do you want it with ice? | 服務生 ▶ 沒問題。請問要加冰塊嗎？

G ▶ No, thanks. | 客人 ▶ 不用，謝謝。

Vocabulary 字彙

01 Unit

02 Unit

03 Unit

04 Unit

05 Unit

06 Unit

07 Unit

08 Unit

1. **delicate** [ˋdɛləkət]　**adj** 形容詞　精美的，雅緻的
The veal we serve is very delicate and therefore it's not good for a spicy sauce.
我們提供的小牛肉清淡可口所以不宜用太多醬料。

2. **ingredient** [ɪnˋgridɪənt]　**n** 名詞　（烹調的）原料
Coconut is a basic ingredient for many of our curry dishes.
椰子是我們很多咖哩菜的基本原料。

3. **seasonal** [ˋsiznəl]　**adj** 形容詞 季節的
We have creative recipes that fully use seasonal vegetables.
我們有善用季節時蔬的創意菜單。

4. **demonstrate** [ˋdɛmənˏstret]　**v** 動詞　示範操作（產品），展示
The chef is now demonstrating how to cook Mapo Tofu.
主廚現在正在示範如何煮麻婆豆腐。

5. **slice** [slaɪs]　**n** 名詞 / v 動詞　薄片，切片，片 / 切成薄片
Would you want me to slice the steak into long thin slices for you, sir?
先生，要我幫你把牛排切成長長的薄片嗎？

6. **dip** [dɪp]　**v** 動詞　沾；浸；泡
Dip the chicken chop quickly in our hot sauce, if you like the spicy taste.
將雞排很快地沾一點我們的辣椒醬，如果你喜歡吃辣。

7. spring onion [sprɪŋ`ʌnjən]　**n** 名詞　青蔥、大蔥

We make our beef salad by combining meat, grapes and spring onions with dressing and toss gently to mix well.

我們將牛肉、葡萄、青蔥和醬汁和在一起然後拌均勻來製作我們的牛肉沙拉。

8. flavorful [`flevɚfəl]　**adj** 形容詞　有風味的

We use flavorful ingredients to make this pizza unique and delicious.

我們用有風味的食材來讓我們的披薩美味且獨特。

In Other Words 這樣說也能通

1. The chef has put mixed seasonal vegetables and prawns in the appetizer.

主廚在這一道開胃菜中放了多種當季蔬菜和明蝦。

★ There are mixed seasonal vegetables and prawns in the appetizer.

★ The appetizer is made of mixed seasonal vegetables and prawns.

2. The prawns in this season are very sweet and tender.

這季的明蝦很鮮甜軟嫩。

★ The prawns are in season and very sweet and tender.

★ The seasonal prawns are very sweet and tender.

3. This is my first time to try Beijing Roast Duck.

這是我第一次嘗試北京烤鴨。

★ I have never tried Beijing Roast Duck before.

★ This is my first time ever to order Beijing Roast Duck.

4. The duck tastes extremely flavorful with spring onions and sweet bean paste.

鴨肉和著甜麵醬和大蔥吃起來非常有風味。

★ The spring onions and sweet bean paste make the duck taste extremely flavorful.

★ The duck meat with spring onions and sweet bean paste has a strong pleasant taste.

Unit 07

Handling Guest Complaints
處理客訴

The food you first served is horrible! 你們提供的餐點糟透了

 Dialogue 停不住對話

W ▶ Waitress　服務生　　**G** ▶ Guest　客人
D ▶ Duty manager　值班經理

G ▶ Excuse me, my steak is overcooked. I wanted it medium rare, but what I have now tastes like a well-done steak.

客人 ▶ 不好意思，我的牛排太熟了。我要的是4、5分熟左右，但現在這份牛排吃起來像全熟。

W ▶ I am terribly sorry, sir. I'll ask our chef to prepare another one for you.

服務生 ▶ 我真的很抱歉，先生。我會請我們主廚再做一份給您。

G ▸ Thanks. In addition, I want to complain that both the broccoli and onion rings are too salty.

客人 ▸ 謝謝。除此之外，我要抱怨綠花椰菜和洋蔥圈都太鹹了。

W ▸ Sorry again. I'll also bring them back to the kitchen. Would you like to order something else?

服務生 ▸ 再次抱歉。我也會把它們拿回廚房。您想要點其他餐點嗎？

G ▸ No, thanks. I would have the same order.

客人 ▸ 不了，謝謝。我要同樣的餐點。

W ▸ Definitely, I'll be back with your orders as soon as possible.

服務生 ▸ 沒問題。我會儘快送上餐點。

W ▸ Sir, here is your steak with broccoli and onion rings. I hope you will enjoy it.

服務生 ▸ 先生這是您的牛排和綠花椰菜洋蔥圈。希望您喜歡。

G ▸ May I speak to your duty manager?

客人 ▸ 可以請你們值班經理來嗎？

W ▸ Certainly. She also likes to talk to you and apologize for it.

服務生 ▸ 當然。她也想和您談談並跟您道歉。

D ▸ Good evening, sir. I am Jane, the duty manager. We are very sorry for the unsatisfactory food we served. Did you find the meal much better this time?

值班經理 ▸ 先生，晚安。我是值班經理Jack。我很抱歉我們提供的食物不符合您的要求。這次重新準備的餐點您滿意嗎？

G ▸ Yes, I did. However, I have to say the food you first served was horrible!

客人 ▸ 滿意。然而我必須説你們第一次出的餐真糟糕。

D ▸ I understand and I will not allow our chef to make such mistakes again. Please accept our sincere apology. We will not charge for the meal and here's a 10% discount coupon for you. We look forward to serving you again in the near future.

值班經理 ▸ 我了解。我不會讓我們主廚再犯一次這樣的錯誤。請接受我們誠摯的道歉。這次的餐點我們就不收費，並提供您一張九折的優待券。我們很期待有再一次服務您的機會。

G ▸ Oh, thanks. I am impressed with the service you provided. I would love to come here again.

客人 ▸ 謝謝。我對你們提供的服務印象深刻。我很樂意再一次來這消費。

D ▸ My pleasure!

值班經理 ▸ 我的榮幸。

Vocabulary 字彙

01 Unit

02 Unit

03 Unit

04 Unit

05 Unit

06 Unit

07 Unit

08 Unit

1. **overcook** [ˌovəˈkʊk] **v** 動詞　使煮過頭，將……煮老
The steak is overcooked, while the vegetables are a little undercooked.
牛排煎得太老了，然而蔬菜炒得有點太生了。

2. **broccoli** [ˈbrɑkəlɪ] **n** 名詞　綠花椰菜
We have a wide selection of fried vegetables such as peas and carrots, broccoli, corn or string beans.
我們有很多炒青菜可供選擇例如豌豆、胡蘿蔔、綠花椰菜、玉米或菜豆。

3. **salty** [ˈsɔltɪ] **adj** 形容詞　鹹的
I think you have made the bacon too salty.
我覺得你們把培根做的太鹹了。

4. **apologize** [əˈpɑləˌdʒaɪz] **v** 動詞　道歉
I apologize for putting too much cream and sugar in your coffee.
我在你咖啡裡放太多奶精和糖，對不起。

5. **unsatisfactory** [ˌʌnsætɪsˈfæktərɪ] **adj** 形容詞　不符合要求的
To be honest, your hot sour soup is unsatisfactory.
老實說，你們的酸辣湯我不滿意。

6. **horrible** [ˈhɔrəb!] **adj** 形容詞　糟透的；可怕的
I was repulsed by the horrible smell.
這種可怕的氣味讓我噁心。

7.**coupon** [`kupɑn]　**n** 名詞　贈券；減價優待券
Tear off this coupon and use it to get 25 % off your next order of side dish.
撕下這張優待券，用它再點一道小菜可打75折。

8.**impress** [ɪm`prɛs]　**v** 動詞　給……極深的印象；使感動
We are impressed by the professionalism of your staff.
我們對你們職員的專業素質印象深刻。

In Other Words 這樣說也能通

1. I wanted it medium rare, but what I have now tastes like a well-done steak.

我要的是4、5分熟左右，但現在這份牛排吃起來像全熟。

☆ You served me a well-done steak, but what I wanted is a medium rare steak.

☆ I wanted my steak medium rare, but what I have now is a well-done steak.

2. We are very sorry for the unsatisfactory food we served.

我很抱歉我們提供的食物不符合您的要求。

☆ We are very sorry that you are not satisfied with the food we served.

☆ We apologize for the unsatisfactory food we served.

3. We will not charge for the meal.

這次的餐點我們就不收費。

☆ Your meal today will be free of charge.

☆ You don't need to pay for the meal. It's on the house.

4. I am impressed with the service you provided.

我對你們提供的服務印象深刻。

☆ The service you provided impressed me.

☆ You have provided a very impressive service.

Unit 07

Handling Guest Complaints
處理客訴

This is not what I ordered! 這不是我點的

 Dialogue 停不住對話 🎧26

W ▸ Waiter 服務生 　**G** ▸ Guest 客人

G ▸ Excuse me, this is not what I ordered! I can't believe you've made such a mistake!

客人 ▸ 不好意思，這不是我點的餐。我不敢相信你會犯這樣的錯誤!

W ▸ I'm so sorry about that. Let me check your order now. You've ordered a Beef Fried Rice.

服務生 ▸ 很抱歉，讓我現在確認您的餐點。您點了一份牛肉炒飯。

G ▸ Yes, and please look at this. You brought me a plate of Beef Fried Noodles.

客人 ▸ 是的，但請看這個。你送來一盤牛肉炒麵。

160

W ▶ I'm so sorry. I'll bring you the right order soon.

服務生 ▶ 真對不起。我會立即把正確的餐點送來。

W ▶ Miss, this is your Beef Fried Rice. Please enjoy it!

服務生 ▶ 小姐，這是您的牛肉炒飯，請享用。

G ▶ Hold on. I've ordered a Beef Fried Rice without spring onions.

客人 ▶ 等一下，我點的是牛肉炒飯不加青蔥。

W ▶ Sorry again! I will bring it back to the kitchen and take out the spring onions.

服務生 ▶ 對不起！我把它送回廚房拿掉青蔥。

G ▶ Thank you, please.

客人 ▶ 謝謝。

After the meal 用餐後

W ▶ Miss, do you save room for some dessert?

服務生 ▶ 小姐，請問要點甜點嗎？

G ▶ No, I am pretty stuffed. I guess I just need a cup of coffee for now. I'd like to have a medium decaf with cream and sugar.

客人 ▶ 不了，我很飽了。我想現在我只需要一杯咖啡。我想要點一個中杯無咖啡因咖啡，加奶精和糖。

W ▶ No problem. I will be right back.

服務生 ▶ 沒問題，我馬上回來。

After half an hour 半小時後

G ▶ Excuse me, I ordered my coffee about 30 minutes ago. Could you please check if it's coming soon?

客人 ▶ 不好意思，我大概30分鐘前點了咖啡。您能否幫我確認咖啡是否快來了？

W ▶ Sorry for the delay. I guess the bar missed your order. Please allow us ten minutes to make your coffee now.

服務生 ▶ 抱歉延誤了。我猜吧檯可能漏了您的訂單。請給我們十分鐘準備您的咖啡。

G ▶ Ten minutes? I'm in a hurry now as I have to return to my office within half an hour. Please cancel my order.

客人 ▶ 十分鐘？我現在趕時間因為我必須在半小時內回到我的辦公室。請取消我的咖啡。

W ▶ Sorry, Miss. Give me 5 more minutes, and I will put your coffee in a to-go cup. It will be free of charge. I am sorry and I will make sure it won't happen again.

服務生 ▶ 小姐很抱歉。請給我五分鐘我會將您的咖啡外帶。這杯咖啡免費招待。我很抱歉，我跟您保證不會再發生這樣的事。

Vocabulary 字彙

1. **fried** [fraɪd] adj 形容詞 油炸的，油煎的
The chef made the stir-fried beef very tender. I like it.
主廚把這牛肉炒得很嫩，我喜歡。

2. **plate** [plet] n 名詞 一盤食物；盤子
My waitress whipped the plate away and left the bill on the table.
我的服務生把盤子撤走並留下帳單在桌上。

3. **dessert** [dɪ`zɝt] n 名詞 餐後甜點
All of our dessert can be served straight from the refrigerator.
我們所有的甜點從冰箱拿出後即可食用。

4. **stuffed** [stʌft] adj 形容詞 吃飽了的
I am so stuffed that I can't take anything more.
我已經飽到吃不下任何東西了。

5. **decaf** [`dikæf] n 名詞 去掉咖啡因的咖啡[茶]
May I have an iced decaf without cream and sugar to go, please?
我可以點一杯無咖啡因咖啡外帶，不加奶精和糖嗎？謝謝。

6. **cream** [krim] n 名詞 奶油；乳脂
Would you like to round off the meal with an ice cream, sir?
先生，您要在餐點結束後來份冰淇淋嗎？

7.**sugar** [`ʃʊgɚ]　**n** 名詞　糖

We provide some dietetic meals which are low in sugar.

我們提供一些含糖量很低的減肥餐點。

8.**delay** [dɪ`le]　**n** 名詞　延誤

The restaurant manager was criticized for his delay in taking care of the guest's complaint.

店經理因延誤處理客人的抱怨而受到批評。

In Other Words 這樣說也能通

01
Unit

02
Unit

03
Unit

04
Unit

05
Unit

06
Unit

07
Unit

08
Unit

1. Miss, do you save room for some dessert?

小姐，請問要點甜點嗎？

☆ Miss, would you like to order dessert?

☆ Miss, are you interested in some dessert?

2. I am pretty stuffed.

我很飽了。

☆ I am already full.

☆ I am full, and can't eat anything more.

3. I'd like to have a medium decaf with cream and sugar.

我想要點一個中杯無咖啡因咖啡，加奶精和糖。

☆ A medium decaf with cream and sugar for me, please.

☆ I'd like to have a medium decaf, and please add cream and sugar in it.

4. It will be free of charge.

這杯咖啡免費招待。

☆ You don't have to pay for the coffee.

☆ It will not be on your bill.

Handling Guest Complaints
處理客訴

7.3 ## You spilled the hot tea all over the table and on my skirt! 你把熱茶灑得滿桌子都是，也灑到我裙子上了

 Dialogue 停不住對話 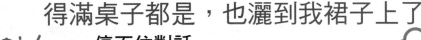 🎧 27

W ▶ Waiter 服務生　**G** ▶ Guest 客人　**M** ▶ Manager 經理

G ▶ Oh, my god! I can't believe what you have done! You spilled the hot tea all over the table and on my skirt!

客人 ▶ 喔，我的天啊！我不敢相信你所做的事！你把熱茶灑得滿桌子都是，也灑到我裙子上了！

W ▶ I'm terribly sorry, ma'am. I will bring you some napkins immediately!

服務生 ▶ 我非常抱歉，女士！我立刻拿給您紙巾。

G ▶ Yes, please hurry up!

客人 ▶ 好的，請趕快！

W ▶ Let me clean it up for you.

服務生 ▶ 請讓我為您清潔。

G ▶ Yes, the table is a mess now. Please give me another table setting.

客人 ▶ 好的，桌子現在很髒。請給我另一份餐具。

W ▶ Certainly, I will be right back with your new set of tableware.

服務生 ▶ 當然，我立即幫您拿一副新的。

M ▶ Good evening, ma'am. I am the manager of this restaurant. This is my business card (The manager hands his business card to the guest).

經理 ▶ 晚安，女士。我是這間餐廳的經理。這是我的名片。（經理把名片地給客人）。

G ▶ Thank you. I think you should improve your staff training as soon as possible.

客人 ▶ 謝謝。我想你們應該盡快改善你們的員工訓練。

M ▶ Thanks very much for your advice. Definitely we will do whatever we can to improve our customer service. Meanwhile, I am very sorry for the inconvenience we've caused you. You have my card, and please send us your dry clean bill and we will pay for that.

經理 ▶ 非常感謝您的建議。當然我們會盡可能改善我們的客戶服務。同時，我很抱歉造成您的不便。你有我的名片，請寄給我你的乾洗帳單，我們會幫您繳費。

01 Unit
02 Unit
03 Unit
04 Unit
05 Unit
06 Unit
07 Unit
08 Unit

G ▸ No, thanks, you don't need to do so.

客人 ▸ 不了，謝謝。你不需要這樣做。

M ▸ If you insist on that, then you will not be charged for your meal this evening. Besides, <u>I would offer you a free dessert.</u>

經理 ▸ 如果您堅持，那麼今晚您的餐點免費。如此之外，我會給您一份免費的甜點。

G ▸ That's very kind of you, sir.

客人 ▸ 先生你人真好。

M ▸ Thank you very much for your understanding.

經理 ▸ 非常感謝您的諒解。

G ▸ By the way, I have another suggestion to make.

客人 ▸ 對了，我有另外一個建議。

M ▸ Yes, please.

經理 ▸ 是的，請説。

G ▸ The music you play here is too loud. <u>I guess most of the people would prefer a quiet dining environment.</u>

客人 ▸ 這裡播放的音樂太大聲了。我猜大多數的人會偏好一個安靜的用餐環境。

01
Unit

02
Unit

03
Unit

04
Unit

05
Unit

06
Unit

07
Unit

08
Unit

 Vocabulary 字彙

1. **spill** [spɪl] ☑ 動詞 溢出；濺出；散落
If you make the cup of coffee too full, it might spill over.
如果你咖啡裝太滿可能會濺出來。

2. **napkin** [`næpkɪn] ⓝ 名詞 餐巾
Please mop up the table quickly with this napkin.
請你迅速用餐巾把桌子擦乾。

3. **tableware** [`teb!ˌwɛr] ⓝ 名詞 餐具
Our range of tableware is decorated with our restaurant logo.
我們所有的餐具都飾有我們餐廳商標。

4. **inconvenience** [ˌɪnkənˈvinjəns] ⓝ 名詞 不便；麻煩，打擾
We apologize for any inconvenience caused during the repairs.
我們為維修期間所造成的不便深感抱歉。

5. **cause** [kɔz] ☑ 動詞 導致，使發生，引起
No, I would not order any dessert. Big meals during the day cause drowsiness.
不，我不點甜點了。白天吃太多會讓人昏昏欲睡。

6. **insist** [ɪnˈsɪst] ☑ 動詞 堅持；堅決認為
I insist on you giving me a straightforward answer.
我一定要你給我一個直接了當地回答。

7.**suggestion** [sə`dʒɛstʃən] **n** 名詞　建議
We welcome any sensible suggestion for improving our customer service.
我們歡迎任何能改善客戶服務的合理建議。

8.**dining** [`daɪnɪŋ] **n** 名詞　進餐
I usually check the seating arrangement before the guests fill into the dining room.
我通常會在客人陸續進入餐廳前確認座位安排。

In Other Words 這樣說也能通

01
Unit

02
Unit

03
Unit

04
Unit

05
Unit

06
Unit

07
Unit

08
Unit

1. Please give me another table setting.

請給我另一份餐具。

✦ May I have another place setting, please?

✦ I would like to have a new set of tableware.

2. I think you should improve your staff training as soon as possible.

我想你們應該盡快改善你們的員工訓練。

✦ I think your staff training should be improved as soon as possible.

✦ I think the first thing you have to do is improve your staff training.

3. I would offer you a free dessert.

我會給您一份免費的甜點。

✦ I would offer you a complimentary dessert.

✦ You will have a complimentary dessert.

4. I guess most of the people would prefer a quiet dining environment.

我猜大多數的人會偏好一個安靜的用餐環境

✦ I think most people would rather have a quiet dining environment.

✦ I think a quiet dining environment is preferable.

Unit 07

Handling Guest Complaints
處理客訴

7.4 **Why is it taking so long? 為什麼要這麼久**

 Dialogue 停不住對話

S ▸ Store manager 店長   **G** ▸ Guest 客人

S ▸ Good evening, ma'am. I am the restaurant manager here. Is there anything I can help you with?

店長 ▸ 晚安，女士。我是這裡的店長。有什麼能為您服務的嗎？

G ▸ Our orders still haven't come yet. We have been waiting for more than 40 minutes. <u>Why is it taking so long?</u> We are starving!

客人 ▸ 我們的餐點還沒來。我們已經點超過40分鐘了。為什麼要這麼久？我們好餓！

S ▸ I'm sorry about that. <u>I thought the waitress who's responsible for your</u>

店長 ▸ 我很抱歉。我以為服務您們的服務生已

table has brought you the meals.

經送餐了。

G ▸ She did, but <u>soon she realized what she delivered was not what we ordered.</u> She said she would be right back, but then she kept us waiting until now.

客人 ▸ 是的，但她立刻發現她送來的餐不是我們點的。她説她會馬上回來，但我讓我們等到現在。

S ▸ Please accept my apology. Let me go and check on your dishes.

店長 ▸ 請接受我的道歉。我現在就去確認您的餐點。

- -

Five minutes later 五分鐘後

S ▸ The waitress is new to the job and we will definitely give her more on-job training. She will bring up your dishes right away. I am very sorry for the inconvenience that we caused. I will like to offer each of you a glass of freshly squeezed orange juice to make up for your loss.

店長 ▸ 這位服務生是新來的，我們一定會給她更多的在職訓練。她會立刻把您的餐點送來。造成您的不便深感歉意。我免費招待你們每一位一杯現榨柳橙汁，以彌補您們的損失。

G ▸ No, thanks. We've ordered a pot of English rose tea.

客人 ▸ 不用了，謝謝。我們有點一壺英式玫瑰茶。

S ▸ OK, I see. Then please allow me to take this item out of your bill.

店長 ▸ 好的，了解。那請讓我免費招待您點的茶。

01 Unit
02 Unit
03 Unit
04 Unit
05 Unit
06 Unit
07 Unit
08 Unit

G ▶ I appreciate that, thank you. By the way, <u>could you do me a favor by turning down the air-conditioner?</u> It's a bit cold here.

S ▶ No problem, I will do so now.

客人 ▶ 感激，謝謝。對了，你可以幫我個忙把冷氣關小嗎？這裡有點冷。

店長 ▶ 沒問題，我現在幫您處理。

Vocabulary 字彙

1. **starving** [`stɑrvɪŋ] adj 形容詞 挨餓的，飢餓的
I am so starving that I would like to order your buffet dinner.
我好餓所以我想點你們的晚餐自助餐。

2. **realize** [`rɪəˌlaɪz] v 動詞 領悟，了解，認識到
I didn't realize that ten people out of this tour group are vegetarians. You should have told me earlier.
我不知道這個旅行團裡有十個人是吃素的。你應該早一點告知我。

3. **apology** [ə`pɑlədʒɪ] n 名詞 道歉；陪罪
The guest wouldn't listen to my apology and insisted on a full refund.
客人不聽我的道歉，堅持要全額退費。

4. **freshly** [`frɛʃlɪ] adv 副詞 新鮮地
A delicious smell of freshly baked bread wafted across the bakery.
麵包店裡飄來一股剛出爐麵包的香味。

5. **squeeze** [skwiz] v 動詞 榨，擠，壓，擰
Part of my every day job is to squeeze orange juice for the guests.
我每天工作的一部分是幫客人榨柳橙汁。

6. **make up** [mek ʌp] v 動詞 彌補
We will do whatever to make up for your loss.
我們會盡可能彌補您的損失。

01 Unit
02 Unit
03 Unit
04 Unit
05 Unit
06 Unit
07 Unit
08 Unit

7. **pot** [pɑt] **n** 名詞 罐；壺；鍋

You have to keep stirring the pot until all the sugar added has melted.

你必須不斷攪拌鍋子直到所有加的糖都融化了。

8. **favor** [`fevɚ] **n** 名詞 善意的行為；恩惠

Actually you have done me a big favor, not the other way around.

事實上你幫了我一個大忙，而不是我幫你。

In Other Words 這樣說也能通

01
Unit

02
Unit

03
Unit

04
Unit

05
Unit

06
Unit

07
Unit

08
Unit

1. Why is it taking so long?

為什麼要這麼久？

✬ Can you tell me why it's taking so long?

✬ I am wondering why it's taking so long.

2. I thought the waitress who's responsible for your table has brought you the meals.

我以為服務您們的服務生已經送餐了。

✬ I thought your waitress has brought up your dishes.

✬ I thought your meals have arrived.

3. Soon she realized what she delivered was not what we ordered.

她立刻發現她送來的餐不是我們點的。

✬ She realized that she served us the wrong order right away.

✬ She immediately found out what she served was not what we ordered.

4. Could you do me a favor by turning down the air-conditioner?

你可以幫我個忙把冷氣關小嗎？

✬ Would you please turn down the air-conditioner for me?

✬ Would you please help me turn down the air-conditioner?

Unit 08

Taking Payment
餐後結帳

Bill, please. 麻煩，買單

 Dialogue 停不住對話　　🎧29

C ▸ Cashier 收銀員　　G ▸ Guest 客人

G ▸ Excuse me, sir. Bill, please! 　　客人 ▸ 先生，不好意思，買單。

C ▸ Certainly, ma'am. Just a moment, please. I'll draw up the bill for you. 　　收銀員 ▸ 好的，女士。請等一下。我開帳單給您。

G ▸ How much is the total? 　　客人 ▸ 總數多少？

C ▸ Your bill comes to NT$6,200 including 10% service charge. 　　收銀員 ▸ 您的帳單金額是台幣6,200元，包含10%的服務費。

G ▸ NT$6,200?! Are you sure? That's way too much. <u>I think you're overcharging me.</u> There must be something wrong.

客人 ▸ 台幣6,200元？你確定嗎？太多了。我想你多收我費用了。一定有錯誤。

C ▸ Here's your bill. Would you like to check on it?

收銀員 ▸ 這是您的帳單，您要檢查一下嗎？

G ▸ Sure, let me see. What is this amount of $2,000 for? And what is the amount of $550 for? I am confused.

客人 ▸ 當然，讓我看一下。這個$2,000金額是什麼？$550的金額是什麼？我搞不清楚。

C ▸ That $2,000 is for the white wine you ordered, and the $550 is for the cheese cake.

收銀員 ▸ $2,000是您們點的白酒的費用，$550是起司蛋糕的金額。

G ▸ White wine and cheese cake? I didn't order them. Did you mix up my bill with other's?

客人 ▸ 白酒和起司蛋糕？我沒有點那些。你是不是把我的帳單和別人的搞混了？

C ▸ Probably. Let me double check it for you. This is the bill for Table 5. Which table are you at?

收銀員 ▸ 有可能，我再幫您確認一下。這是五桌的帳單。您們是坐哪一桌？

G ▸ We are at Table 6.

客人 ▸ 我們是六桌。

C ▸ Oh, I am so sorry. Let me reprint your bill.

收銀員 ▸ 很抱歉，讓我重新列印您的帳單。

01 Unit
02 Unit
03 Unit
04 Unit
05 Unit
06 Unit
07 Unit
08 Unit

G ▶ That's ok. How much does it come to now?

客人 ▶ 沒關係，那現在金額是多少？

C ▶ It's NT$2,640. Do you want me to go through the bill with you?

收銀員 ▶ 總價是台幣2,640元。要不要我們再一起核對帳單？

G ▶ If it's not too bothering.

客人 ▶ 如果不是太麻煩的話。

C ▶ Definitely not. You've ordered three set meals. Each is for $800. 800 times 3 equal 2,400, plus 10% service charge. Therefore, the total amount is $2,640.

收銀員 ▶ 當然不會。您們點了三份套餐。每一份800元。800乘以3等於2400，加上10%的服務費。所以總數是2640元。

G ▶ Yes, that's correct. Thank you. <u>May I pay by credit card?</u>

客人 ▶ 是的，正確。可以用信用卡付款嗎？

C ▶ Sorry, ma'am. We only accept cash.

收銀員 ▶ 很抱歉，女士。我們只接受現金。

G ▶ OK, here you are. NT$3,000.

客人 ▶ 好的，這裡是台幣3,000元。

C ▶ Here is your change.

收銀員 ▶ 這是您的找零。

G ▶ Thank you.

客人 ▶ 謝謝。

Vocabulary 字彙

1. **bill** [bɪl]　**n** 名詞　帳單
Please sign the bill now and the waiter will return with your order soon.
請在帳單上簽名，服務生很快會送上您的餐點。

2. **draw up** [drɔ ʌp]　**v** 動詞　起草；制訂
Should I draw up your bill for you?
要我幫您結帳嗎？

3. **overcharge** [ˋovɚˋtʃɑrdʒ]　**v** 動詞　對……索價太高
Not only did the restaurant overcharge me, but they hadn't served us well.
這間餐廳不僅要價太高，對我們的服務也不周到。

4. **amount** [əˋmaʊnt]　**n** 名詞　總數；總額
Our cashier always verifies that the payment and invoice amount match.
我們的收銀員都會核對付款和發票上的金額是否一致。

5. **mix up** [mɪks ʌp]　**v** 動詞　拌和；弄混
I'll get you the right order. Sorry about the mix-up.
我去給您拿您點的菜。抱歉我們搞錯了。

6. **bother** [ˋbɑðɚ]　**v** 動詞　煩擾、打擾
Don't bother to refill my water; I am not thirsty.
不用麻煩幫我倒水；我不渴。

01 Unit
02 Unit
03 Unit
04 Unit
05 Unit
06 Unit
07 Unit
08 Unit

7.**set meal** [sɛt mil]　**n** 名詞　套餐；客飯
All our set meals come with soup or salad, dessert, and a drink.
我們所有的套餐都附湯、沙拉、甜點、和飲料。

8.**change** [tʃendʒ]　**n** 名詞　零錢；找零
This is $2,000. Keep the change!
這是兩千元。零錢不用找了。

In Other Words 這樣說也能通

1. I'll draw up the bill for you.

   我開帳單給您。

   ✦ Let me prepare your bill now.
   ✦ Let me settle your bill now.

2. Your bill comes to NT$6200 including 10% service charge.

   你的帳單金額是台幣6200元，包含10%的服務費。

   ✦ The total charge comes to NT$6200 including 10% service charge.
   ✦ The total amount of your bill is NT$6200, which includes 10% service charge.

3. I think you're overcharging me.

   我想你多收我費用了。

   ✦ I guess you charge me too much.
   ✦ I think the amount you charge me is too high.

4. May I pay by credit card?

   可以用信用卡付款嗎？

   ✦ Can I use credit card to pay for it?
   ✦ Do you accept credit cards?

Unit 08

Taking Payment
餐後結帳

8.2

Would you like to separate the check? 你們要各自付帳嗎

 Dialogue 停不住對話

C ▶ Cashier 收銀員　G ▶ Guest 客人

C ▶ Good evening, sir. How may I help you?　收銀員 ▶ 晚安，先生。有什麼能為您服務的？

G ▶ Yes, I'd like to settle our bill. How much is it?　客人 ▶ 我想買單。多少錢？

C ▶ I'll figure it out for you. The bill adds up to NT$858. <u>Would you like to separate the check, sir?</u>　收銀員 ▶ 我幫您計算。帳單總數是台幣858元。您們要各自付帳嗎？

G ▶ <u>The dinner is on me</u>. I'll take care of it. However, are you sure the total amount is correct? We ordered two sets of chicken curry rice. Shouldn't it be NT$780?

客人 ▶ 晚餐我請，我會付。不過你確定總數是對的嗎？我們點了兩份咖哩雞飯。不是應該是台幣780元嗎？

C ▶ A 10% service charge has been added to your bill.

收銀員 ▶ 10%的服務費包含在帳單裡。

G ▶ Can you tell me approximately how much the service charge is?

客人 ▶ 你可以告訴我服務費大概是多少嗎？

C ▶ Wait a moment. Let me calculate it now. It's NT$78.

收銀員 ▶ 稍等一下，我現在計算。台幣78元。

G ▶ Oh, I see. Thank you. May I use a traveler's check to pay for it?

客人 ▶ 我知道了，謝謝你。 我可以用旅行支票付帳嗎？

C ▶ I am afraid that we don't take traveler's checks in this restaurant, but we do accept cash and credit card.

收銀員 ▶ 我們餐廳不收旅行支票，但我們接受現金和信用卡。

G ▶ Well, I'll pay in cash then. Here's NT$1,000.

客人 ▶ 那我付現。這裡是1,000元。

C ▶ I'll be back soon with your receipt and change.

收銀員 ▶ 我馬上拿您的收據和找零來。

G ▶ All right. Thank you.

客人 ▶ 好的。謝謝！

C ▸ Here are your change and your receipt. <u>Thanks for coming and look forward to seeing you again in the near future.</u>

收銀員 ▸ 這裡是您的找零及收據。謝謝您的光臨,期待在近期內能再看到您們。

G ▸ We will. We are both very satisfied with the meals and service you provide here. By the way, I'd like to change some U.S. dollars into NT dollars. Do you know where I should go?

客人 ▸ 會的。我們對您提供的餐點和服務都非常滿意。對了,我想把一些美金換成台幣,你知道我該去哪換嗎?

C ▸ <u>There is foreign exchange at the front desk of this hotel.</u>

收銀員 ▸ 這個飯店的櫃台有外幣兌換。

G ▸ Great. Thanks for telling me.

客人 ▸ 太好了,謝謝您告知。

Vocabulary 字彙

1.**settle** [`sɛt!] **v** 動詞　支付，結算
Let's settle the bill up together.
我們一起付帳吧。

2.**figure out** [`fɪgjɚ aʊt] **v** 動詞　演算出、計算出；想出、理解、明白
I can't figure out why the bill comes to such a high amount.
我無法理解為何帳單金額會這麼高？

3.**curry** [`kɝɪ] **n** 名詞　咖喱
I will recommend you order curry rice instead of curry noodles as rice makes an excellent complement to a curry dish.
我會建議你點咖哩飯而不是咖哩麵，因為咖哩配上米飯是最棒。

4.**calculate** [`kælkjə‚let] **v** 動詞　計算
Let me calculate the total cost of the ten set meals you ordered.
讓我計算一下你們點的十份套餐的總金額。

5.**traveler's check** [`trævlɚz tʃɛk] **n** 名詞　旅行支票
Cash or traveler's check is the only form of payment in this restaurant.
收費以現金和旅行支票為限。

6. **accept** [əkˋsɛpt] **v** 動詞　接受

I owe you an apology for the unsatisfactory service we provided.

我為服務不周向您道歉。

7. **receipt** [rɪˋsit] **n** 名詞　發票；收據

I am going to make out a receipt for you.

我開一張收據給你。

8. **foreign exchange** [ˋfɔrɪn ɪksˋtʃendʒ] **ph** 片語　外幣兌換

If you want to pay in USD, you can refer to the foreign exchange rate list over there.

如果你要用美金付帳，你可以參考那邊的外匯匯率價一覽表。

In Other Words 這樣說也能通

1. Would you like to separate the check, sir?

   你們要各自付帳嗎？

   ✮ Would you like to split the check, sir?

   ✮ Would you like to go Dutch?

2. The dinner is on me.

   晚餐我請。

   ✮ The dinner is my treat.

   ✮ I will pick up the check for tonight.

3. Thanks for coming and look forward to seeing you again in the near future.

   謝謝您的光臨，期待在近期內能再看到您們。

   ✮ Thanks for coming and hope soon we'll have another chance to serve you.

   ✮ Thanks for your coming and hope to see you soon,

4. There is foreign exchange at the front desk of this hotel.

   這個飯店的櫃台有外幣兌換。

   ✮ You can exchange money at the front desk of this hotel.

   ✮ The front desk of this hotel offers foreign exchange service.

01 Unit

02 Unit

03 Unit

04 Unit

05 Unit

06 Unit

07 Unit

08 Unit

Unit 08

Taking Payment
餐後結帳

Can I use this voucher to pay for the meals? 我可以用這個餐券付帳嗎

 Dialogue 停不住對話

S ▸ Server 服務生　**G** ▸ Guest 客人

S ▸ Was everything to your satisfaction?

服務生 ▸ 一切滿意嗎？

G ▸ Yes, we enjoyed the meals very much. However, we had waited for almost one hour before a table was available.

客人 ▸ 是的，餐點很好吃。但我們等了快一個小時才有位子。

S ▸ Sorry for keep you waiting. I strongly recommend you to book your table in advance. This is our business card and you can call this

服務生 ▸ 很抱歉讓您等待。我強烈建議你事先訂位。這是我們店卡，下次你可以打這個訂位

reservation hotline next time.	專線。

G ▸ Thanks, we will.

客人 ▸ 謝謝，我們會的。

S ▸ The restaurant will be closed in half an hour. May I settle your bill now?

服務生 ▸ 餐廳半小時內就要打烊了。可以幫您買單嗎？

G ▸ Sure. How much is it?

客人 ▸ 當然，多少錢？

S ▸ Just a moment, please. Here is your bill, ma'am. And the total amount is $4,800

服務生 ▸ 請等一下。先生，這是您的帳單，總金額是台幣4,800元。

G ▸ Can I use this voucher to pay for the meals?

客人 ▸ 我可以用這個餐券付費嗎？

S ▸ Certainly, ma'am, but I'm afraid it will not cover the total cost of the meal.

服務生 ▸ 當然可以，女士。但恐怕這個餐券不夠付總金額。

G ▸ I know this voucher is only worth $3,000. Can I use my credit card to pay for the difference?

客人 ▸ 我知道這餐券只價值3,000元。我可以用信用卡付差額嗎？

S ▸ Absolutely, we accept Visa, MasterCard, and American Express.

服務生 ▸ 當然，我們收VISA卡，萬事達卡，和美國運通。

G ▸ Perfect! I'll pay with my MasterCard.

客人 ▸ 太好了，我用我的萬事達卡付。

01 Unit
02 Unit
03 Unit
04 Unit
05 Unit
06 Unit
07 Unit
08 Unit

S ▶ Sorry, ma'am. The card you gave me doesn't work. Do you have another card?

服務生 ▶ 女士，對不起。你給我的卡不能刷。你有另一張卡嗎？

G ▶ No, I don't. I will pay by cash then. Here are $2,000.

客人 ▶ 沒有，那我付現好了。這裡是2,000元。

S ▶ No problem. I will be right back with the change.

服務生 ▶ 沒問題，我馬上找零給你。

- -

S ▶ Ma'am, here is your change. Thank you very much.

服務生 ▶ 女士，這是您的找零。謝謝您。

G ▶ Wait a second. <u>I think the amount of change is not correct.</u>

客人 ▶ 等一下，找零的金額不對。

S ▶ I'm very sorry, ma'am. May I see your bill again, please?

服務生 ▶ 很抱歉，我可以再看一次您的帳單嗎？

G ▶ Here. Go ahead.

客人 ▶ 在這裡，請。

S ▶ May I ask how much change I gave you, ma'am?

服務生 ▶ 女士，可以請問我剛剛找多少錢給您嗎？

G ▶ The change should be $200, but you gave me $100 instead.

客人 ▶ 應該找零200元，但你給我100元。

S ▶ I apologize for the mistake I made. Here is the right amount.

服務生 ▶ 我為我犯的錯誤道歉。這裡是正確的金額。

Vocabulary 字彙

1. **satisfaction** [ˌsætɪsˈfækʃən] **n** 名詞　滿意，滿足
   As a server, I do my best to give the customers satisfaction.
   作為一個服務生，我盡力讓顧客滿意。

2. **in advance** [ɪn ədˈvæns] **ph** 片語　預先
   You might have to book a table a week or more in advance.
   你可能需要一週前或更早前就要預訂位子。

3. **voucher** [ˈvaʊtʃɚ] **n** 名詞　券 ex:shopping voucher（消費券）；
   gift voucher（禮券）
   You can use this voucher for an American Breakfast.
   你可以用這張餐券點美式早餐。

4. **cover** [ˈkʌvɚ] **v** 動詞　（錢）足夠付
   Is the voucher value sufficient to cover the total cost of the meals?
   這張餐券的面額足夠支付所有餐點嗎？

5. **worth** [wɝθ] **adj** 形容詞　有（……的）價值，值……
   This French restaurant is well worth a visit.
   這家法國餐廳非常值得光顧。

6. **difference** [`dɪfərəns] **n** 名詞　差額
We offer 10% discount of all our lunch specials this week, and that means there will be about NTD1000 difference in the total amount of your meals.
本週我們所有特別午餐都打九折，也就是說今天你們餐點的總金額會有大約1,000元的差額。

7. **absolutely** [`æbsə͵lutlɪ] **adv** 副詞　絕對地
It was absolutely the worst food I have ever had.
這絕對是我吃過最糟糕的食物。

8. **go ahead** [go ə`hɛd] **ph** 片語　去吧
A:May I clean your table now?
B:Sure, go ahead.
A:現在可以幫你清理桌子嗎？
B:當然，做吧。

In Other Words 這樣說也能通

1. Was everything to your satisfaction?

一切滿意嗎？

✦ Are you satisfied with everything?

✦ Does everything meet your expectations?

2. We had waited for almost one hour before a table was available.

我們等了快一個小時才有位子。

✦ We had waited for almost one hour for a table.

✦ You had kept us waiting for nearly one hour before we got a table.

3. I strongly recommend you to book your table in advance.

我強烈建議你事先訂位。

✦ My advice will be booking your table in advance.

✦ I strongly recommend you make a reservation.

4. I think the amount of change is not correct.

找零的金額不對。

✦ I think you gave me a wrong amount of change.

✦ The amount of change you gave me is wrong.

Unit 08

Taking Payment
餐後結帳

Can I pay in US dollars? 我可以用美金付嗎

 Dialogue 停不住對話 🎧 32

S ▸ Server 服務生   **G** ▸ Guest 客人

G ▸ Excuse me.

客人 ▸ 服務生,請來一下!

S ▸ Yes, sir. How may I help you?

服務生 ▸ 是的,先生,有什麼可以為您服務的?

G ▸ Can you wrap up this Red-cooked Pork and Wonton Soup for us, please?

客人 ▸ 可以幫我們把紅燒豬肉和餛飩湯打包嗎?

S ▶ Certainly. How was everything? Did you enjoy your lunch?

服務生 ▶ 當然,餐點如何?好吃嗎?

G ▶ Yes, <u>for me, the dishes are all very tasty, but they are a bit too salty for my wife.</u>

客人 ▶ 對我來說每道菜都很美味,但我太太覺得有一點太鹹了。

S ▶ Oh, sorry to hear that. I will let our chef know.

服務生 ▶ 很遺憾。我會轉告我們主廚。

S ▶ Here are your Red-cooked Pork and Wonton Soup to go. <u>Are you ready for the</u> check, <u>sir?</u>

服務生 ▶ 這是您要打包的紅燒豬肉和餛飩湯。請問要買單了嗎?

G ▶ Yes, please.

客人 ▶ 是的,請。

S ▶ Here is the check. The total comes to $2,200.

服務生 ▶ 這是帳單。總金額是2,200元。

G ▶ Excuse me. The amount sounds not right. See, you listed Wonton Soup and jasmine tea here. <u>The soup and tea are included in the lunch special</u> combo, <u>aren't they?</u>

客人 ▶ 不好意思,這金額聽起來不對。你看,你把餛飩湯和茉莉花茶也算進去了。湯品和茶不是包含在午餐特餐組合裡嗎?

S ▶ I am afraid not. Today is Saturday and here it says, "Saturdays and Sundays not included".

服務生 ▶ 恐怕不是,今天是週六。這裡有寫"不包含週六週日"。

G ▶ I see, but that still doesn't make

客人 ▶ 我了解了,但總

01 Unit

02 Unit

03 Unit

04 Unit

05 Unit

06 Unit

07 Unit

08 Unit

$2,200. I have showed the hostess my VIP card and that should have offered me 10% discount of the total cost.

數也不該是2,200元。我有給你們領檯員看我的VIP卡，這樣應該可以打九折才對。

S ▶ Oh, sorry. I didn't know that. Can you show me the VIP card again?

服務生 ▶ 喔，對不起，我不知道你有VIP卡。可以再給我看一次嗎？

G ▶ No problem. Here you go.

客人 ▶ 沒問題，在這裡。

S ▶ Thank you. Could you allow me some time to reprint your check?

服務生 ▶ 謝謝，可以給我一些時間重印您的帳單嗎？

G ▶ Sure, go ahead.

客人 ▶ 當然，去吧。

S ▶ The total now comes to $980. How would you like to pay?

服務生 ▶ 總數是1980元。您要如何付款？

G ▶ I will pay by cash. Oh, sorry. I just realized that I don't have enough NT dollars with me. Can I pay in US dollars?

客人 ▶ 我付現。喔，不好意思，我發現我現在身上沒有足夠的台幣。我可以用美金付嗎？

S ▶ That's no problem. I will ask the cashier to prepare the check in US dollars.

服務生 ▶ 沒問題，我會請收銀員以美元計價的帳單。

G ▶ Thanks very much for your help.

客人 ▶ 非常謝謝您的幫忙。

Vocabulary 字彙

1. **wrap up** [ræp ʌp] Ⓥ 動詞　包裹、包好、裹住
What is a word to describe something you use to wrap up the meat?
你用來包肉的那個東西叫做什麼？

2. **red-cooked** [rɛd kʊkt] 🔲 形容詞　紅燒的
Our chef's specials today are red-cooked beef, honey ham, and sweet and sour fish.
今天我們的主廚推薦菜色為紅燒牛肉、蜜汁火腿和糖醋魚。

3. **check** [tʃɛk] 🔲 名詞　【美】（餐廳的）帳單
Would you double check if the amount on the check is correct?
您可以檢查一下帳單上的金額是否正確嗎？

4. **combo** [`kɑmbo] 🔲 名詞　組合；套餐
I would like to have one BigMac Combo and two happy meals.
我想點一份大麥克套餐和兩份兒童餐。

5. **jasmine** [`dʒæsmɪn] 🔲 名詞　茉莉花
Oolong tea and jasmine tea are the bestselling tea at our restaurant.
烏龍茶和茉莉花茶是我們餐廳最暢銷的茶款。

6. **discount** [`dɪskaʊnt] 🔲 名詞　折扣
We offer 15% discount for cash payment.
現金付款我們打八五折。

7. **realize** [ˋrɪəˌlaɪz] **v** 動詞　領悟，了解，認識到

I didn't realize how expensive this dinner was going to be.

我沒想到這份晚餐這麼貴。

8. **cashier** [kæˋʃɪr] **n** 名詞　收銀員、出納

I think the cashier made a mistake and short-changed me.

我想收銀員弄錯了，少找我錢。

In Other Words <u>這樣說也能通</u>

01
Unit

1. For me, the dishes are all very tasty, but they are a bit too salty for my wife.

對我來說每道菜都很美味，但我太太覺得有一點太鹹了。

☆ I enjoyed all the dishes, but my wife thinks they are a bit too salty.

☆ All the dishes are very tasty for me, but a bit too salty for my wife.

02
Unit

03
Unit

2. Are you ready for the check, madam?

請問要買單了嗎？

☆ Should I draw up a bill for you now?

☆ Would you like to pay now?

04
Unit

3. The soup and tea are included in the lunch special combo, right?

湯品和茶不是包含在午餐特餐組合裡嗎？

☆ The lunch special combo includes the soup and tea, right?

☆ I thought the soup and tea are free if I order the lunch special combo?

05
Unit

06
Unit

4. The total now comes to $1,980.

總數現在是1,980元。

☆ The bill now comes to $1,980.

☆ The total is now $1,980.

07
Unit

08
Unit

2 Part

Cooking Area

內場

Unit 09

Food Preparation- Vegetables and Fruits
食材處理 – 蔬菜與水果

9.1

We have to prepare cabbages for the beef soup. 我們要準備牛肉湯要用的高麗菜

  *Dialogue* 停不住對話 🎧 33

C ▶ Commis Cook 廚師助理 **V** ▶ Vegetable Chef 蔬菜廚師

V ▶ We have to prepare cabbages for the beef soup.

蔬菜廚師 ▶ 我們要準備牛肉湯要用的高麗菜。

C ▶ How many heads of cabbages do we need?

廚師助理 ▶ 我們需要幾顆高麗菜？

V ▶ Two.

蔬菜廚師 ▶ 兩顆。

C ▶ OK. How should I cook the cabbages?

廚師助理 ▶ 好的，要怎麼煮呢？

V ▶ First of all. Cut the cabbage in half and then cook it in the boiled water. By the way, don't forget to add a pinch of baking soda to the water.

蔬菜廚師 ▶ 首 先， 把 兩顆高麗菜切半然後水煮。對了，不要忘了加少許小蘇打粉到水裡。

C ▶ Why do we need to add that?

廚師助理 ▶ 為 什 麼 要 加小蘇打粉？

V ▶ Baking soda can help keep the original color of the cabbage.

蔬菜廚師 ▶ 小 蘇 打 粉 可以讓高麗菜在水煮過程中保持原色。

C ▶ I see. I learn something again today.

廚師助理 ▶ 了 解， 今 天又學到東西了。

V ▶ <u>After you have done cooking, you can wash lettuce.</u>

蔬菜廚師 ▶ 你 煮 好 高 麗菜後就可以洗萵苣。

C ▶ Should we soak the lettuce in salted water first?

廚師助理 ▶ 要 先 把 萵 苣泡在鹽水裡嗎？

V ▶ Yes, for about half an hour.

蔬菜廚師 ▶ 要， 大 概 半小時。

C ▶ After the lettuce is washed, should I cut them up?

廚師助理 ▶ 萵 苣 洗 好 後要把它切碎嗎？

V ▶ No, <u>lettuce will be used for making salads and therefore we need whole leaves.</u> Besides lettuce, we will also add celery to the salad.

蔬菜廚師 ▶ 不， 萵 苣 是用來做沙拉，所以我們需要完整的葉子。除了萵苣，我們也會加芹菜在沙拉裡。

09
Unit

10
Unit

11
Unit

12
Unit

C ▶ OK, I will wash that later. I remember we are also making stews for tonight.

廚師助理 ▶ 好的，我待會會洗芹菜。我記得今天晚上我們也要做燉菜。

V ▶ Yes, you are right. I plan to use the peas for it.

蔬菜廚師 ▶ 是的，你說對了。我計畫用豌豆做燉菜。

C ▶ Are we using frozen or canned peas?

廚師助理 ▶ 我們要用冷凍還是罐裝的豌豆？

V ▶ <u>Neither frozen nor tinned peas will taste good.</u> I insist on using fresh peas.

蔬菜廚師 ▶ 冷凍或罐裝的都不好吃。我堅持用新鮮豌豆。

C ▶ I see. So we must shell them.

廚師助理 ▶ 了解，所以我們必須把青豆剝出來。

V ▶ Correct. Please ease the peas from the pods into a colander.

蔬菜廚師 ▶ 正確。請把青豆剝出來倒進濾碗裡。

C ▶ We have different types of colander. Which one are we using? It's quite confusing.

廚師助理 ▶ 我們有不同種的濾碗，我們要用哪一種？我常搞不懂。

V ▶ Take the one with big holes and the little peas will fall out of the bottom.

蔬菜廚師 ▶ 拿那個上面有很大濾孔的，這樣小的豌豆就會從底部掉出來。

C ▶ Got you!

廚師助理 ▶ 懂了！

 Vocabulary 字彙

1. **cabbage** [ˋkæbɪdʒ] **n** 名詞　高麗菜，甘藍菜
Please cut the cabbage into fine long shreds.
請將高麗菜切成又細又長的絲。

2. **lettuce** [ˋlɛtɪs] **n** 名詞　萵苣
The so-called green salad has only green vegetables, such as lettuce and cucumber.
所謂的綠色沙拉指的是只有綠色的蔬菜，例如萵苣和小黃瓜。

3. **soak** [sok] **v** 動詞　浸泡
Leave the dried beans to soak in water overnight.
把這些乾豆子在水裡泡一夜。

4. **celery** [ˋsɛlərɪ] **n** 名詞　芹菜
The celery is fresh and crisp. Our guests will like it a lot.
這芹菜新鮮脆嫩。我們客人一定很喜歡。

5.**stew** [stju] **n** 名詞　燉肉，燜菜；燉煮的食物
Would you please divide the meat evenly and boil it in a stew?
你可以把那塊肉均勻切成小塊放到燉菜裡煮嗎？

6.**frozen** [`frozn] **adj** 形容詞　冰凍的；結冰的
Can you now place the frozen rolls on a greased baking tray?
你現在可以把冷凍肉捲放在抹了油的烤盤上嗎？

7.**canned** [kænd] **adj** 形容詞　裝成罐頭的
You have to rinse the canned sauerkraut first in order to reduce the sodium content.
你必須先沖洗罐裝的德國泡菜以降低鈉的含量。

8.**colander** [`kʌləndɚ] **n** 名詞　濾器；濾鍋
After the cabbage is boiled, strain off the water through a colander.
高麗菜煮開後，用濾鍋把水濾掉。

In Other Words 這樣說也能通

1. How should I cook the cabbages?

要怎麼煮高麗菜呢？

⭐ What should I do with the cabbages?

⭐ Can you tell me how to cook the cabbages?

2. After you have done cooking, you can wash lettuce.

你煮好高麗菜後就可以洗萵苣。

⭐ Please wash the lettuce after you are done with cabbages.

⭐ After the cabbages are cooked, you can wash the lettuce.

3. Lettuce will be used for making salad and therefore we need whole leaves.

萵苣是用來做沙拉，所以我們需要完整的葉子。

⭐ We need whole leaves of lettuce for making salad.

⭐ We will use whole leaves of lettuce when we make salad.

4. Neither frozen nor tinned peas will taste good.

冷凍或罐裝的豌豆都不好吃。

⭐ Both frozen and tinned peas won't taste good.

⭐ I don't like frozen and tinned peas.

Food Preparation- Vegetables and Fruits
食材處理 － 蔬菜與水果

9.2

Can you peel the onion and then chop them finely? 你可以將洋蔥去皮然後把它們切成細末嗎

 Dialogue 停不住對話  (34)

C ▶ Commis Cook 廚師助理   **V** ▶ Vegetable Chef 蔬菜廚師

V ▶ Let's now prepare some potatoes, onions, carrots, and tomatoes.

蔬菜廚師 ▶ 我們現在來準備馬鈴薯，洋蔥，胡蘿蔔，和番茄。

C ▶ There is a whole sack of potatoes over there. How many do we need?

廚師助理 ▶ 那裏有一整袋馬鈴薯。我們需要幾顆？

V ▶ I think we need them all. Please wash them carefully.

蔬菜廚師 ▶ 我想全部都要。請仔細清洗它們。

C ▶ Yes, madam. I will do it right away.

廚師助理 ▶ 是的，現在就洗。

V ▶ Don't forget to scrub them with a brush.

蔬菜廚師 ▶ 不要忘記用刷子把表皮刷乾淨。

C ▶ And then?

廚師助理 ▶ 然後呢？

V ▶ Use that potato peeler to peel them.

蔬菜廚師 ▶ 用削皮刀把皮削掉。

C ▶ OK, how should I cut them?

廚師助理 ▶ 好的，要怎麼切呢？

V ▶ Cut them into dices. We are making soup with the potatoes.

蔬菜廚師 ▶ 把它們切丁。這些馬鈴薯要用來煮湯。

V ▶ Can you peel the onion and then chop them finely?

蔬菜廚師 ▶ 你可以將洋蔥去皮然後把它們切成細末嗎？

C ▶ We also need finely chopped onions for the soup?

廚師助理 ▶ 我們煮的湯也需要用到切細的洋蔥？

V ▶ Yes.

蔬菜廚師 ▶ 是的。

C ▶ How about these carrots? I also dice them?

廚師助理 ▶ 那這些胡蘿蔔呢？也切丁嗎？

V ▶ No, you cut the carrots into sticks. The carrots will be used for the salad. You also need to boil them in salted water.

蔬菜廚師 ▶ 不，把胡蘿蔔切成條狀。這些胡蘿蔔是做沙拉用的。也需要放到鹽水裡煮。

C ▶ I am finished the potatoes, onions, and carrots.

廚師助理 ▶ 馬鈴薯，洋蔥和胡蘿蔔都準備好了。

V ▶ Then wash the tomatoes, please.

蔬菜廚師 ▶ 然後請洗番茄。

C ▶ Should I reomve the stem?

廚師助理 ▶ 要把中間的蒂去掉嗎？

V ▶ Yes, please. Next put the tomatoes into the boiling water for about fifteen seconds and then put them immediately in the ice water.

蔬菜廚師 ▶ 是的，請。然後把番茄放進滾水裡煮大約15秒，再立刻放進冰水裡。

C ▶ Why?

廚師助理 ▶ 為什麼？

V ▶ <u>So we can peel the tomatoes easily if we do so.</u>

蔬菜廚師 ▶ 這樣就可以輕易地把皮去掉。

Vocabulary 字彙

1. **sack** [sæk]　n 名詞　袋、粗布袋、麻袋、一袋的量
Oh, my god. This sack of rice was bit by rats and insects.
喔，我的天啊。這包米被老鼠和蟲咬了。

2. **scrub** [skrʌb]　v 動詞　用力擦洗；揉
You cannot scrub tableware with detergent.
不能用洗衣粉擦洗餐具。

3. **brush** [brʌʃ]　v 動詞 / n 名詞　刷、刷子
Can you use the stiff brush to clean the sink?
你可以用那個硬毛刷來清理水槽嗎？

4. **peel** [pil]　v 動詞　削去……的皮，剝去……的殼
Should I peel the pears and remove the cores now?
現在要把梨子削皮去核了嗎？

5. **dice** [daɪs]　n 名詞 / v 動詞　骰子狀小方塊；將（蔬菜等）切成小方塊
Rinse red chili and dice finely.
把辣椒洗淨切幼粒。

6. **chop** [tʃɑp]　v 動詞　切細，剁碎
Chop the mushrooms and quarter the potatoes.
把蘑菇剁碎，然後把馬鈴薯切成四半。

7. **stick** [stɪk]　n 名詞　棒狀物
We will put some sticks of celery into salad.
我們會放幾根芹菜棒到沙拉裡。

8. **boil** [bɔɪl] **V** 動詞　烹煮

Boil the peas, and add garlic and lemon juice.

把豌豆放進開水裡煮，並加大蒜和檸檬汁。

In Other Words 這樣說也能通

1. Use that potato peeler to peel them.

   用削皮刀把皮削掉。

   ☆ We can use the peeler to peel the potatoes.
   ☆ We can peel the potatoes with the peeler.

2. We are making soup with the potatoes.

   這些馬鈴薯要用來煮湯。

   ☆ One of the ingredients we use for the soup is potato.
   ☆ We will use potatoes to make the soup.

3. We also need finely chopped onions for the soup?

   我們煮的湯也需要用到切細的洋蔥？

   ☆ We also need to chop onions finely in order to make the soup.
   ☆ We will use diced onions for the soup.

4. So we can peel the tomatoes easily if we do so.

   這樣就可以輕易地把皮去掉。

   ☆ Doing so can make us easily peel the tomatoes.
   ☆ We can peel the tomatoes by doing so.

09
Unit

10
Unit

11
Unit

12
Unit

Unit 09

Food Preparation- Vegetables and Fruits
食材處理 – 蔬菜與水果

9.3 It will take one hour to fully defrost the meat. 肉可能需要一小時才能完全解凍

 Dialogue 停不住對話

H ▸ Commis Cook 廚師助理   V ▸ Vegetable Chef 蔬菜廚師

V ▸ We are making stuffed green peppers tonight.

蔬菜廚師 ▸ 我們今晚要做青椒鑲肉。

C ▸ Yes, sir. I will wash these green peppers first.

廚師助理 ▸ 是。我先洗這些青椒。

V ▸ You can wash them in the sink. Don't forget to use the sink stopper.

蔬菜廚師 ▸ 你可以用水槽洗。記得用塞子把排水孔塞住。

C ▸ OK. Then I will cut the green peppers open and remove the seeds?

廚師助理 ▸ 好的。 然後我把青椒切開然後去籽嗎？

V ▸ Correct! Then we will stuff the peppers with meat together. Take out one pack of ground pork from the fridge for me, please.

蔬菜廚師 ▸ 正確！你完成後我們一起把肉塞進青椒裡。請幫我從冰箱拿一包豬絞肉出來。

C ▸ Sure. Sorry, somehow I can't find any ground pork in the fridge.

廚師助理 ▸ 好的。 對不起，我怎麼在冰箱裡沒看到絞肉？

V ▸ That's weird. I remember I put it there last night. Wait, maybe I've put it in the walk-in freezer.

蔬菜廚師 ▸ 奇怪，我記得我昨晚放在那裏啊。等一下，我可能放進冷凍庫裡。

C ▸ Let me check. Yes, there it is. It will take one hour to fully defrost the meat.

廚師助理 ▸ 我看一下，有，在冷凍庫裡。肉可能需要一小時才能完全解凍。

V ▸ No worries. We still have plenty of time, and we can prepare fruits for now.

蔬菜廚師 ▸ 別擔心，我們還有很多時間。我們現在可以準備水果。

C ▸ The fruits we need for the banquet tonight?

廚師助理 ▸ 今晚晚宴需要的水果嗎？

V ▸ Yes, please bring me five mangoes, half a watermelon, four

蔬菜廚師 ▸ 是的，請給我五個芒果，半個西

bananas, and three apples.

瓜，四根香蕉，和三個蘋果。

C ▶ Should I remove the pit from the mango?

廚師助理 ▶ 要把芒果的核去掉嗎？

V ▶ Yes, please. Then peel and mash up the bananas. Slice the watermelon and apples. Remember to soak the apple slices in the salted water.

蔬菜廚師 ▶ 是的，請。然後把香蕉皮剝掉，把香蕉搗成泥狀。把西瓜和蘋果切片。記得把蘋果切片浸在鹽水裡。

C ▶ Yes, sir. How do I serve them?

廚師助理 ▶ 好的，那要怎麼擺盤呢？

V ▶ We serve watermelon with apple slices in the largest plate.

蔬菜廚師 ▶ 西瓜和蘋果切片一起放在最大的盤子裡。

C ▶ How about the mashed bananas?

廚師助理 ▶ 那香蕉泥呢？

V ▶ We will use that for the fruit salad later.

蔬菜廚師 ▶ 待會做水果沙拉時才需要用到。

Vocabulary 字彙

1. **stuffed** [stʌft]　adj 形容詞　有餡的
Would you like to order stuffed tomatoes?
你要點番茄鑲肉嗎？

2. **sink** [sɪŋk]　n 名詞　洗滌槽，水槽
It is important that the draining board, sink and plug hole are regularly disinfected.
滴水板，水槽，和塞孔定期消毒是很重要的。

3. **seed** [sid]　n 名詞　種子，籽
You have to remove the seeds of the cherries before you put them in the pie.
櫻桃去籽後才能做成派。

4. **fridge** [frɪdʒ]　n 名詞　冰箱
We always put what's left in a covered container in the fridge.
我們都會把剩下的食材裝入有蓋的容器然後放進冰箱。

5. **freezer** [`frizɚ]　n 名詞　冷凍庫
The freezer is the place we put frozen food.
冷凍庫是用來保存冷凍食品。

6. **defrost** [di`frɔst]　v 動詞　解凍
Make sure you defrost the beef completely before you cook it.
牛肉在烹煮前一定要完全解凍。

09
Unit

10
Unit

11
Unit

12
Unit

7. **mango** [`mæŋgo]　n 名詞　芒果

Do you think we should add several slices of mango in the fruit salad?

你覺得我們要加幾片芒果在沙拉裡嗎？

8. **slice** [slaɪs]　v 動詞　把……切成薄片

Can you slice the cooking apple finely and slice the meat thickly?

你可以把烹調用的蘋果切成薄片，然後把肉切厚片嗎？

In Other Words 這樣說也能通

1. I will cut the green peppers open and remove the seeds?

   我把青椒切開然後去籽嗎？

   ☆ Should I cut the green peppers open and take out the seeds?

   ☆ The green peppers should be cut open and the seeds be removed?

2. Then we will stuff the peppers with meat together.

   你完成後我們一起把肉塞進青椒裡。

   ☆ I will stuff the peppers with meat with you after you are done.

   ☆ After you are done, let's stuff the peppers with meat together.

3. It will take one hour to fully defrost the meat.

   肉可能需要一小時才能解凍。

   ☆ We might have to wait for one hour before the meat can be fully defrosted.

   ☆ It might take one hour for the meat to fully defrost.

4. The fruits we need for the banquet tonight?

   今晚晚宴需要的水果嗎？

   ☆ Are the fruits for the banquet tonight?

   ☆ These are the fruits we will use for tonight's banquet?

Unit 09

Food Preparation- Vegetables and Fruits
食材處理－蔬菜與水果

9.4

After you drain them, butter and salt these carrots. 瀝乾之後，再將胡蘿蔔抹上奶油和鹽

 Dialogue 停不住對話 🎧36

CC ▶ Commis Cook 廚師助理　　CF ▶ Chef 主廚

CC ▶ What should I do with these carrots?

廚師助理 ▶ 我要怎麼料理這些胡蘿蔔？

CF ▶ Are they cooked?

主廚 ▶ 煮過了嗎？

CC ▶ Yes, I just poached them.

廚師助理 ▶ 有，我剛水煮過。

CF ▶ Good. Now put them in a colander.

主廚 ▶ 很好。現在把它們放進濾鍋中。

CC ▶ To drain them?

廚師助理 ▶ 為了把水瀝乾嗎？

CF ▶ Yes, you are right! <u>After you drain them, butter and salt these carrots.</u>

主廚 ▶ 是，你說對了。瀝乾之後，再將胡蘿蔔抹上奶油和鹽。

CC ▶ I butter and salt the carrots while they are in the colander or I do so after I take them out?

廚師助理 ▶ 是在濾鍋裡就抹還是拿出來以後再抹？

CF ▶ Take them out first.

主廚 ▶ 先拿出來。

CC ▶ OK, the carrots are buttered and salted.

廚師助理 ▶ 胡蘿蔔已抹上奶油和鹽了。

CF ▶ Thank you. Leave them there for about twenty minutes.

主廚 ▶ 謝謝，先放置約20分鐘。

CC ▶ OK. What should I do next?

廚師助理 ▶ 好的，接下來要做什麼？

CF ▶ <u>We have some potato strips in the fridge. Can you take out some for me?</u>

主廚 ▶ 冰箱裡還有一些馬鈴薯條。可以幫我拿一些出來嗎？

CC ▶ Yes. Are we making French fries?

廚師助理 ▶ 好，我們要做炸薯條嗎？

CF ▶ You bet! Put the potato in a frying basket, and then put the frying

主廚 ▶ 沒錯！把馬鈴薯放到油炸籃裡，再把油

basket in the deep fryer.　　　　　　炸籃放到油炸鍋裡。

CF ▸ Let's make a salad now.

主廚 ▸ 我們現在做沙拉。

CC ▸ What should we start with?

廚師助理 ▸ 我們要從哪一種材料開始準備？

CF ▸ The spring onions. Wash them first.

主廚 ▸ 青蔥，先洗。

CC ▸ And then?

廚師助理 ▸ 然後呢？

CF ▸ Trim off both ends and split the spring onions down the middle.

主廚 ▸ 把頭尾兩端切掉，然後從中間切開。

CC ▸ OK, I will.

廚師助理 ▸ 好的，我會。

CF ▸ Then we will make some garlic butter for the salad dressing.

主廚 ▸ 然後我們要做沙拉醬要用到的大蒜奶油醬。

CC ▸ I know how to make a garlic butter. I have done that before.

廚師助理 ▸ 我知道怎麼做大蒜奶油醬，我以前做過。

CF ▸ Tell me how you are going to make it.

主廚 ▸ 告訴我你會怎麼做？

CC ▸ I will peel the garlic first, and then crush and grind it. At then mix

廚師助理 ▸ 我會先把大蒜壓扁再磨碎。最後

the garlic with butter.

把蒜泥和奶油拌在一起。

CF ▶ You forgot to add the salt to the garlic!

主廚 ▶ 你忘了要加鹽。

CC ▶ Oh, yes. Thanks for reminding me.

廚師助理 ▶ 喔。 對，謝謝你提醒。

 Vocabulary 字彙

1. **poach** [potʃ] **V** 動詞 水煮；清蒸；煨燉
Can you put on a pan of water to simmer and gently poach the eggs?
你可以放一鍋水用小火煮蛋嗎？

2. **drain** [dren] **V** 動詞 排水；濾乾
Drain the beans thoroughly and save the stock for soup, please.
請把豆子徹底濾乾，然後把濾出的豆汁留下做湯。

3. **split** [splɪt] **V** 動詞 劈開；切開
If the chicken is fairly small, you may simply split it in half.
如果雞比較小，你就把它切成兩半就好。

4. **garlic** [ˋgɑrlɪk] **n** 名詞 大蒜；蒜頭
I usually add generous amount of garlic to add flavor.
我通常加比較多的蒜來提味。

5. **dressing** [ˋdrɛsɪŋ] **n** 名詞　（烤雞等用的）填料；（拌沙拉等用的）調料

You can make the dressing by mixing the ingredients in that bowl.

你可以把碗裡的原料混成醬料。

6. **crush** [krʌʃ] **v** 動詞　壓碎，壓壞；碾碎；榨

Can you mix these vegetables in a bowl and crush them with a potato masher?

你可以把這些蔬菜在碗裡攪拌，然後用絞馬鈴薯器把他們搗碎嗎？

7. **grind** [graɪnd] **v** 動詞　磨（碎）；碾（碎）

You can store the peppercorns in that container and grind the pepper when needed.

你可以把那個胡椒粒放在那個容器，需要用時再磨成粉。

8. **mix** [mɪks] **v** 動詞　使混和，攪和[（+with）]

Mix the meat with the onion, carrot, garlic, and chili power.

把肉和洋蔥，胡蘿蔔，大蒜和辣椒粉攪拌在一起。

In Other Words 這樣說也能通

1. What should I do with these carrots?

我要怎麼料理這些胡蘿蔔？

⭐ How should I cook these carrots?

⭐ Can you tell me how I should do with these carrots?

2. After you drain them, butter and salt these carrots.

瀝乾之後，再將胡蘿蔔抹上奶油和鹽。

⭐ Butter and salt these carrots after you drain them.

⭐ You drain them first and then butter and salt these carrots.

3. We have some potato stripes in the fridge. Can you take out some for me?

冰箱裡還有一些馬鈴薯片。可以幫我拿一些出來嗎？

⭐ Can you take out some potato stripes in the fridge for me?

⭐ The potato stripes are in the fridge. Please take some out for me.

4. Then we will make some garlic butter for the salad dressing.

然後我們要做沙拉醬要用到的大蒜奶油醬。

⭐ We are making some garlic butter for the salad dressing.

⭐ Let's make some garlic butter which will be used in the salad dressing.

Unit 10

Cooking-Soups
烹飪 — 湯品

French Onion Soup 法式洋蔥湯

 Dialogue 停不住對話

CC ▶ Commis Cook 廚師助理　**CF** ▶ Chef 主廚

CF ▶ Ted, I will teach you how to make French Onion Soup today. <u>It is one of our most popular soups.</u>

主廚 ▶ Ted，今天我會教你做法式洋蔥湯。這是我們很受歡迎的湯品之一。

CC ▶ Yes, I can't wait to learn how to make it.

廚房助理 ▶ 好 的， 我迫不及待想學。

CF ▶ <u>The main ingredients for this soup are onions, butter, beef broth,</u>

主廚 ▶ 這道湯的主要材料有洋蔥，奶油，牛肉

228

cheese, and French bread. Angela has sliced ten onions yesterday. You can just cook them in butter.

清湯，起司，和法式麵包。Angela 昨天已經把十個洋蔥切好了。你現在可以把奶油加進去和洋蔥一起炒。

09 Unit

CC ▶ Over low heat?

廚房助理 ▶ 用小火嗎？

CF ▶ Yes, please, and stir constantly.

主廚 ▶ 是的，不時攪拌一下。

10 Unit

CC ▶ I think the onions are pretty much done.

廚房助理 ▶ 我想洋蔥差不多好了。

CF ▶ Add the beef broth and water. Also put some bay leaves, pepper, and thyme in it to add flavor.

主廚 ▶ 把牛肉清湯和水加進去。也加一點月桂葉、胡椒、和百里香來增加風味。

11 Unit

CC ▶ OK, done. I will now heat the soup to a boil?

廚房助理 ▶ 好的。做好了。然後把湯加熱煮滾嗎？

12 Unit

CF ▶ Fine, but remember to lower the heat when the soup is boiling. Then cover the pan and keep at a simmer for about twenty minutes.

主廚 ▶ 可以。記得湯滾後要調成小火，然後蓋上蓋子小火慢燉約20分鐘。

CC ▶ What should I do in the meantime?

廚房助理 ▶ 那這段時間我要做什麼？

CF ▶ You can toast the French

主廚 ▶ 你可以烤法國麵

bread. It takes just about twenty minutes.

After twenty minutes…

包。烤麵包的時間剛好也是20分鐘。

20分鐘後……

CF ▶ Can you pour the soup into the bowls? I will top each with a slice of toasted French bread.

主廚 ▶ 你可以把烤好的法國麵包放進碗裡嗎？我要把洋蔥湯淋下去。

CC ▶ Yes, sir. What should I do with the cheese? Did I forget to add it when I make the soup base?

廚房助理 ▶ 是的。那這些起司呢？我是不是在做湯底時忘了加？

CF ▶ No, don't worry. We just need to sprinkle grated cheese on top of the soup now.

主廚 ▶ 不，別擔心。我們只需要現在把起司灑在湯上。

CC ▶ Oh, I see. So are we done our French onion soup yet?

廚房助理 ▶ 喔，我知道了。所以洋蔥湯做好了？

CF ▶ Pretty much. The final step is to put the bowls in the salamander oven just before serving the soup.

主廚 ▶ 差不多了。最後一個步驟就是在湯端上桌之前先把碗放進烤箱保溫。

Vocabulary 字彙

1. **broth** [brɔθ] **n** 名詞 （用肉、蔬菜等煮成的清淡的）湯
I usually use corn flour to thicken the broth.
我通常用玉米粉把湯變濃稠。

2. **stir** [stɝ] **v** 動詞 攪拌
You have to stir the sauce fully before you pour it over the top of the salad.
你要先充分攪拌醬汁才能把它淋在沙拉上。

3. **flavor** [`flevɚ] **n** 名詞 味，味道
Fry quickly to seal in the flavor of the meat.
快速把肉煎一下就可以鎖住肉的美味。

4. **simmer** [`sɪmɚ] **v** 動詞 煨，燉
Can you now reduce the heat and simmer the sauce gently for 10 minutes?
你可以現在把火關小然後把調味醬用小火慢燉10分鐘嗎？

5. **toast** [tost] **v** 動詞 烤麵包片
Toast the bread lightly on both sides.
把麵包兩面稍微烤一下。

6. **pour** [por] **v** 動詞 倒，灌，注
Pour the mixture into the cake tin and bake for 40 minutes.
把混和物倒進烤模，然後烤40分鐘。

7.**sprinkle** [`sprɪŋkl̩] **v** 動詞　灑，噴淋；撒

Place the fish on the chopping block and sprinkle it with lemon juice and pepper.

把魚放在沾板上然後撒上檸檬汁和胡椒。

8.**salamander** [`sælə͵mændɚ] **n** 名詞　輕便烤箱

Can you take out those soup bowls from the salamander?

你可以把那些湯碗從烤箱中拿出來嗎？

In Other Words 這樣說也能通

1. It is one of our most popular soups.

這是我們很受歡迎的湯品之一。

☆ It is our best-selling soup.

☆ This soup is very popular among our guests.

09
Unit

2. The main ingredients for this soup are onions, butter, beef broth, cheese, and French bread.

這道湯的主要材料有洋蔥，奶油，牛肉清湯，起司，和法式麵包。

☆ We mainly use onions, butter, beef broth, cheese, and French bread to make the soup.

☆ This soup is mainly made of onions, butter, beef broth, cheese, and French bread.

10
Unit

11
Unit

3. Remember to lower the heat when the soup is boiling.

記得湯滾後要調成小火。

☆ Once the soup is boiling, reduce the heat.

☆ Turn down the heat once the soup is boiling.

12
Unit

4. Are we done our French onion soup yet?

洋蔥湯做好了？

☆ Is our French soup done?

☆ Is the French onion soup ready to serve?

Unit 10

Cooking- Soups
烹飪 — 湯品

10.2

Eel Soup 鰻魚湯

 Dialogue 停不住對話　

CC ▶ Commis Cook　廚師助理　　**CF ▶** Chef　主廚

CC ▶ Are we going to make Eel Soup today?

廚房助理 ▶ 我們現在要做鰻魚湯嗎？

CF ▶ Yes, that's right. <u>Have you boiled the ham bone with water in a large saucepan?</u>

主廚 ▶ 是的。你有把帶骨火腿在大型長柄煮鍋中用水煮嗎？

CC ▶ Yes, for about two hours.

廚房助理 ▶ 有，煮了大概兩小時。

CF ▸ Did you remember to keep the pan partly covered?

主廚 ▸ 你記得不要完全蓋上蓋子嗎？

CC ▸ Yes, I did.

廚房助理 ▸ 有的。

09 Unit

CF ▸ Good. Now we add the fruits and vegetables, and keep at a simmer gently until they are soft.

主廚 ▸ 很好。現在我們加入水果和蔬菜，用小火繼續慢慢燉煮到其變軟。

10 Unit

CC ▸ Yes, sir.

廚房助理 ▸ 好的。

CF ▸ While we are making the soup base, we can prepare the eel. Do you still remember how to do it?

主廚 ▸ 我們在做湯底的同時可以處理鰻魚。你還記得怎麼做嗎？

11 Unit

CC ▸ Yes, skin the eel and rub it with salt and then cut it into chunks. Put the eel into another pan, and add water, bay leaf, peppercorns, and rice wine in it.

廚房助理 ▸ 記得。要去掉鰻魚的皮並抹上鹽，然後切塊放進另一個鍋中。加入水、月桂葉，胡椒粒，和米酒。

12 Unit

CF ▸ <u>The water must cover the eel completely.</u>

主廚 ▸ 水要完全將鰻魚覆蓋。

CC ▸ Yes, <u>thanks for reminding me.</u>

廚房助理 ▸ 是的，謝謝您的提醒。

CF ▸ Place the pan over high heat, and bring it to a boil. Then we lower the heat and simmer gently until the eel meat is tender. It might take about thirty minutes.

主廚 ▸ 把鍋子放在大火上煮到沸騰。然後我們轉小火慢燉，直到鰻魚變軟。大概煮三十分鐘。

After thirty minutes… 30分鐘後……

CF ▶ OK, I think the eel is now nice and tender. Can you remove the ham bone from the soup base now?

主廚 ▶ 好的，現在鰻魚應該已經軟嫩了。你可以把帶骨火腿從湯底中取出嗎？

CC ▶ Yes, and I will cut it into chunks?

廚房助理 ▶ 好的，要切塊嗎？

CF ▶ Yes, please, set the meat chunks aside. Mix the butter and flour into a smooth paste and then cut it into tiny pieces.

主廚 ▶ 是的，把切好的肉塊先放在一旁。把奶油和麵粉揉成一個均勻的麵糰，然後把麵團分成小塊。

CC ▶ Are these small pieces used to thicken the soup base?

廚房助理 ▶ 這些小麵糰是用來把湯變得濃稠的嗎？

CF ▶ Yes, you got it. After the soup is slightly thickened, add the finely chopped herbs and the cooked eels with its soup in it.

主廚 ▶ 是的，你説對了。湯變得有點黏稠之後，把切碎的香料和煮好的鰻魚肉塊和湯汁加進湯裡。

CC ▶ How about the ham bone meat?

廚房助理 ▶ 那這些帶骨火腿肉塊呢？

CF ▶ Add it in as well. Then we just need to season the soup and we are done!

主廚 ▶ 也加進去。然後我們只要把湯調味就完成了。

Vocabulary 字彙

1. **eel** [il]　🅝 名詞　鰻魚
In Tainan, there were many restaurants specializing in eel noodles.
在台南有很多專門賣鱔魚麵的餐廳。

2. **saucepan** [`sɔs͵pæn]　🅝 名詞　（長柄有蓋的）平底深鍋
Fill the saucepan with water and bring to a boil.
把平底湯鍋加滿水煮沸。

3. **skin** [skɪn]　🆅 動詞　剝……的皮；去……的殼
You have to skin the onions first.
你必須先剝洋蔥皮。

4. **rub** [rʌb]　🆅 動詞
Can you rub the fish with salt and pepper?
你可以把魚抹上鹽和胡椒嗎？

5. **chunk** [tʃʌŋk]　🅝 名詞　（肉、木材等的）大塊，厚片
Can you chop that chunk of meat into six pieces?
你可以把那一大塊肉切成六塊嗎？

6. **paste** [pest]　🅝 名詞　（做糕點用的）麵糰
We have to stir the flour and milk to a stiff paste first.
我們必須先把麵粉和牛奶攪成很黏的麵糊。

7. **thicken** [`θɪkən]　🆅 動詞　變濃；使變厚
Don't worry; the pudding will thicken as it cools.
別擔心，布丁涼了就會變濃稠。

8. **chop** [tʃɑp] Ⅴ動詞 劈；砍；剁

You've got to chop up the pork before frying it.

你必須先把豬肉剁碎再炒。

In Other Words 這樣說也能通

1. Have you boiled the ham bone with water in a large saucepan?

   你有把帶骨火腿在大型長柄煮鍋中用水煮嗎？

   ⭐ Have you used the large saucepan to boil the ham bone in water?

   ⭐ Has the ham bone been boiled in water in a large saucepan?

2. The water must cover the eel completely.

   水要完全將鰻魚覆蓋。

   ⭐ The eel must be covered completely in water.

   ⭐ The water must completely cover the eel.

3. Thanks for reminding me.

   謝謝您的提醒。

   ⭐ Thanks for your reminder.

   ⭐ Thank you for reminding.

4. Are these small pieces used to thicken the soup base?

   這些小麵糰是用來把湯變得濃稠的嗎？

   ⭐ We will thicken the soup base by using these small pieces?

   ⭐ The soup base can be thickened by these small pieces?

Unit 10

Cooking- Soups
烹飪－湯品

10.3   Chicken Soup 雞湯

 Dialogue 停不住對話   39

CC ▶ Commis Cook 廚師助理   **CF** ▶ Chef 主廚

CF ▶ The chicken soup we are making now is probably far more complicated than you thought.

主廚 ▶ 我們現在要做的雞湯可能比你想像的要複雜許多。

CC ▶ Does that mean that we will use lots of ingredients to make it?

廚房助理 ▶ 你的意思是我們要用很多材料煮它嗎？

CF ▶ Yes, besides boned chicken, we also need different kinds of

主廚 ▶ 是的，除了去骨雞肉，我們還需要不同

vegetables such as onions, parsley, lentils, and tomatoes.

種類的蔬菜例如洋蔥、荷蘭芹、扁豆，和番茄。

CC ▶ I saw you also asked John to prepare some rice, flour, eggs, butter and lemon juice. Are they also for the soup?

廚房助理 ▶ 我看到你也叫John準備一些米飯、麵粉、蛋、奶油、和檸檬汁。它們也是用來煮湯的嗎？

CF ▶ Yes. As for the seasoning, we need salt, freshly grounded black pepper, sweet paprika, and powdered saffron.

主廚 ▶ 是的，至於調味，我們需要鹽巴，新鮮研磨的黑胡椒，甜椒粉，和番紅花粉。

CC ▶ Woo, that's really a lot.

廚房助理 ▶ 哇，真的很多。

CF ▶ Now we have all the ingredients we need. Let's start cooking the soup.

主廚 ▶ 現在我們需要的材料都有了。現在開始煮湯。

CC ▶ What should I start with?

廚房助理 ▶ 要從哪裡開始？

CF ▶ Use the large saucepan to stir-fry the boned chicken with the butter, onion, and parsley for about five minutes.

主廚 ▶ 用大的長柄煮鍋炒去骨雞肉，加入奶油、洋蔥、和荷蘭芹，翻炒大約五分鐘。

CC ▶ How do I season it?

廚房助理 ▶ 要怎麼調味？

CF ▶ You can add some sweet paprika, powdered saffron, pepper and salt.

主廚 ▶ 你可以加一些甜椒粉、翻紅花粉、胡椒和鹽巴。

CC ▶ Got it. <u>May I know the exact amount of sweet paprika and powered saffron?</u>

廚房助理 ▶ 知道了。你可以告訴我甜椒粉和番紅花要加多少嗎？

CF ▶ It depends on the amount of soup we make. Today we are making the soup for thirty people, and we probably need 4 teaspoons of sweet paprika and 2 teaspoons of powdered saffron.

主廚 ▶ 這取決於我們要做的湯的量。今天我們要做三十人份的湯，大概需要四茶匙的甜椒粉和兩茶匙的翻紅花粉。

CC ▶ I see. What's next?

廚房助理 ▶ 知道了，然後呢？

CF ▶ Add the water, lentils, tomatoes and lemon juice in the pan and cook for one and half hours. After that, we put the rice in and cook for another 15 to 20 minutes.

主廚 ▶ 把水，扁豆，番茄，和檸檬汁加入鍋中煮一個半小時。之後把米飯加入再煮15到20分鐘。

CC ▶ Woo, <u>the soup really takes a long time to cook.</u>

廚房助理 ▶ 哇，這湯真的很花時間熬煮。

CF ▶ Yes, and that's why our chicken soup are so tasty.

主廚 ▶ 是的，這也就是我們的雞湯會這麼美味的原因。

Vocabulary 字彙

1. **boned** [bond]   adj 形容詞   去骨的
The boned chicken claws are our best selling products.
去骨雞爪是我們賣最好的產品。

2. **lentil** [`lɛntɪl]   n 名詞   扁豆
We fry the noodles with the meats, the spinach, and the lentil.
我們用肉、菠菜、和扁豆炒麵。

3. **seasoning** [`siznɪŋ]   n 名詞   調味；調味料，佐料
The leaves of this plant can be used as a seasoning.
這種植物的葉子可作為調味料。

4. **powdered** [`paʊdəd]   adj 形容詞   變成粉末的，粉末（狀）的
Do we put powdered milk into the curry?
我們要在咖哩裡加奶粉嗎？

5. **saffron** [`sæfrən]   n 名詞   番紅花
Can I tell the guests the secret of our saffron sauce?
我可以跟客人說我們的番紅花醬秘方嗎？

6. **stir- fry**   v 動詞   翻炒；拌炒
Stir-fry the shred shallots with some olive oil.
把切絲的紅蔥頭用橄欖油拌炒。

7. **teaspoon** [`ti͵spun]   n 名詞   茶匙；小匙
Give me one teaspoon of cinnamon.
給我一茶匙的肉桂。

8. **tasty** [`testɪ] adj 形容詞 美味的;可口的

We fry the duck with pig fat to make the meat tasty.

我們用豬油炒鴨肉讓肉更美味。

 In Other Words 這樣說也能通

1. Besides boned chicken, we also need different kinds of vegetables such as onions, parsley, lentils, and tomatoes.

除了去骨雞肉,我們還需要不同種類的蔬菜例如洋蔥、荷蘭芹、扁豆,和番茄。

   ☆ Besides boned chicken, we need different kinds of vegetables such as onions, parsley, lentils, and tomatoes.

   ☆ In addition to boned chicken, we also need such vegetables as onions, parsley, lentils, and tomatoes.

2. As for the seasoning, we need salt, freshly grounded black pepper, sweet paprika, and powdered saffron.

至於調味,我們需要鹽巴,新鮮研磨的黑胡椒,甜椒粉,和番紅花粉。

   ☆ We season it with salt, freshly grounded black pepper, sweet paprika, and powdered saffron.

   ☆ We need salt, freshly grounded black pepper, sweet paprika, and powdered saffron for the seasoning.

3. May I know the exact amount of sweet paprika and powered saffron?

你可以告訴我甜椒粉和番紅花要加多少嗎？

☆ May I know how much sweet paprika and powered saffron I should add in?

☆ Can you tell me the exact amount of sweet paprika and powered saffron?

4. The soup really takes a long time to cook.

這湯真的很花時間熬煮。

☆ It really takes time to cook the soup.

☆ Cooking the soup is very time-consuming.

Unit 10

Cooking-Soups
烹飪 — 湯品

| 10.4 | **Creamy Sweet Corn Soup** 玉米濃湯 |

 Dialogue 停不住對話 40

CC ▶ Commis Cook 廚師助理　**CF** ▶ Chef 主廚

CC ▶ Are we using canned corn for tonight's creamy sweet corn soup?

廚房助理 ▶ 我們要用玉米罐頭來做今晚的玉米濃湯嗎？

CF ▶ No, I don't like the taste of canned corn. We will use fresh corn for the soup. The corns this season are very sweet. It takes much more time if we use fresh corns, but that will make our soup different from

主廚 ▶ 不，我不喜歡加工玉米的味道。我們會用新鮮玉米煮湯。這季的玉米非常甜。用新鮮玉米煮要多花很多時間，但這會讓我們的湯

others'.

與眾不同。

CC ▶ I see. How many corns do we need?

廚房助理 ▶ 了解。 我們需要幾根玉米？

CF ▶ Take ten ears please. Remove husks and silks from corn, and then use a knife to take corn kernels off.

主廚 ▶ 請拿十根。將外皮及玉米鬚拔乾淨，然後用刀子把玉米粒切下。

CC ▶ Done. Then I will cook these corn kernels with water?

廚房助理 ▶ 好了。 然後水煮這些玉米粒嗎？

CF ▶ Yes, please, and add some sugar. Remember to reserve three to four teaspoons of corn for garnish.

主廚 ▶ 是的，然後加些糖。記得留三到四匙的玉米裝飾用。

CC ▶ OK, I will. What's next?

廚房助理 ▶ 好 的， 然後呢？

CF ▶ Blend the rest well to a smooth paste. Drain the corns to remove the skin. This step is optional, but I do this always.

主廚 ▶ 把剩餘的玉米粒混和攪成很爛的玉米糊。然後把玉米糊脫水並去除玉米薄膜。這步驟你可選擇要做或不做，但我都會做。

CC ▶ I will do so as well because it will make the soup taste better.

廚房助理 ▶ 我 也 會 做因為這可讓湯更美味。

CF ▶ I agree. And then add milk and water to cook the corn kernels and bring to the boil.

主廚 ▶ 我同意。然後加入牛奶和水煮玉米粒到沸騰。

CC ▶ Will we also thicken the soup?

廚房助理 ▶ 我們也要勾芡嗎？

CF ▶ Yes, definitely. Dissolve two teaspoons of flour in water. And then whisk it slowly into the soup.

主廚 ▶ 當然。用兩茶匙的麵粉溶入水中，然後緩慢地將它滴入湯中。

CC ▶ Should I constantly stir the soup while I do so?

廚房助理 ▶ 我要同時持續攪拌湯嗎？

CF ▶ Yes, please. Then we add super, salt and pepper and mix them well. Garnish with the corn kernels.

主廚 ▶ 是的。最後我們加入糖，鹽，和胡椒，充分攪拌。用玉米粒裝飾。

CC ▶ May I also put some parsley in it?

廚房助理 ▶ 可以加一點和荷蘭芹嗎？

CF ▶ That's a good idea.

主廚 ▶ 好主意。

Vocabulary 字彙

1. **corn** [kɔrn]　n 名詞　玉米
Our corn flour has been ground very fine.
我們的玉米粉已經被磨得很細。

2. **creamy** [ˋkrimɪ]　adj 形容詞　含奶油的；似乳脂
We make a rich and creamy soup with meat, fish, and shellfish.
我們用肉、魚和貝類做濃郁的奶油濃湯。

3. **processed** [ˈprəʊsest]　adj 形容詞　加工過的
We try our best not to use processed ingredients.
我們盡量不用加工食材。

4. **strand** [strænd]]　n 名詞　線；繩
We use these strands to wrap the zongzi.
我們用這些細繩包粽子。

5. **kernel** [ˋkɝn!]　n 名詞　（果核或果殼內的）仁
Our kernel bread tastes fragrant and sweet.
我們的果仁麵包又香又甜。

6. **blend** [blɛnd]　v 動詞　（烹飪時）在某物中加入其他成分使之混合
Melt the butter and then blend in the flour, and then blend the eggs and milk together.
先把奶油融化加入麵粉，然後把蛋和奶混和攪在一起。

7. **dissolve** [dɪ`zɑlv] Ⓥ 動詞　使溶解；使融化

Dissolve the chocolate in the top of a double boiler.

在雙層蒸鍋的上層鍋內溶解巧克力。

8. **stir** [stɝ] Ⓥ 動詞　攪拌

You have to stir the sauce constantly to prevent it lumping.

你必須持續攪拌醬汁避免它結塊。

In Other Words 這樣說也能通

1. It takes much more time if we use fresh corns, but that will make our soup different from others'.

用新鮮玉米煮要多花很多時間，但這會讓我們的湯與眾不同。

⭐ Using fresh corns takes much more time, but it also differentiates our soup from others'.

⭐ Fresh corns can make our soup different from others even though they take time to cook.

2. I will cook these corn kernels with water?

我要水煮這些玉米粒嗎？（口語中以加強疑問口吻，而省略倒裝的問句）

⭐ Should I boil these corn kernels?

⭐ Should I water cooking these corn kernels?

3. Should I constantly stir the soup while I do so?

我要同時持續攪拌湯嗎？

⭐ Meanwhile should I constantly stir the soup?

⭐ Should I keep stirring the soup while I do so?

4. May I also put some parsley in it?

可以加一點荷蘭芹嗎？

⭐ How about putting some parsley in?

⭐ Can I add in some parsley?

Unit 11

Cooking- Main Courses
烹飪 - 主菜

| 11.1 | **Marinated Fish Cooked in Olive Oil** 橄欖油香煎魚排 |

Dialogue 停不住對話

CC ▶ Commis Cook 廚師助理   **CF** ▶ Chef 主廚

CF ▶ Have you marinated the halibut steak?

主廚 ▶ 你已醃好比目魚排了嗎？

CC ▶ Yes, I've put all the ingredients for the marinade in a shallow bowl, added the fish in, and set them aside for 6 hours.

廚房助理 ▶ 是 的 ， 我把所有的醃料放在一個淺碗中，把魚放進去，然後擱置六小時。

CF ▶ Good. Did you turn the fish steak over occasionally?

主廚 ▶ 很好。你有不時翻動魚排嗎？

CC ▶ Yes, this time I didn't forget about doing so.

廚房助理 ▶ 有，這次我沒忘記要這樣做。

CF ▶ Great. Now preheat the oven to 200 degrees Fahrenheit.

主廚 ▶ 很好。現在把烤箱重新加熱到華氏200度。

CC ▶ Yes. What's next?

廚房助理 ▶ 好的，然後呢？

CF ▶ Remove the fish from the marinade.

主廚 ▶ 把魚從醃料中拿出來。

CC ▶ Pat it dry with paper towels?

廚房助理 ▶ 用餐巾紙拍乾嗎？

CF ▶ Yes, please.

主廚 ▶ 是的。

CC ▶ How about the marinade? <u>Are we still using it later?</u>

廚房助理 ▶ 那這些醃料呢？我們待會還要用嗎？

CF ▶ Yes, reserve one tablespoon of it.

主廚 ▶ 要，留一大匙備用。

CC ▶ OK.

廚房助理 ▶ 好的。

CF ▶ <u>Now scale and bone the halibut.</u>

主廚 ▶ 現在把比目魚去鱗然後去骨。

CC ▶ Yes, done. Should I cut it into pieces?

廚房助理 ▶ 好的，完成了。要把它切片嗎？

CF ▶ Let me see. The halibut steak today is bigger than usual. I will say we cut it into fourths.

主廚 ▶ 我看一下。今天的比目魚比平時的大。我想就把它切成四等分吧。

CC ▶ No problem. Now we will cook the pieces of fish in the casserole?

廚房助理 ▶ 沒問題。現在我們把魚片放在砂鍋裡煮嗎？

CF ▶ Yes, heat about two teaspoon of oil in it first.

主廚 ▶ 是的，先加兩茶匙的油進去。

CC ▶ Yes, next?

廚房助理 ▶ 好的。接下來？

CF ▶ Arrange a layer of fish in the bottom of the casserole. Can you also mix the olive oil with the saffron, ginger, and one tablespoon of marinade we reserved earlier, and pour it over the fish?

主廚 ▶ 把魚片鋪在烤鍋底層。你現在可以把橄欖油和番紅花、薑、還有剛剛保留下來一大匙的醃醬一起攪拌，然後淋在魚上嗎？

CC ▶ Yes, done. I will cover the casserole now, and simmer over very low heat.

廚房助理 ▶ 好的，完成了。我現在把砂鍋蓋上，然後用小火慢燉。

CF ▶ Just simmer for five minutes.

主廚 ▶ 用小火慢慢煮五分鐘就好。

CC ▶ No problem.

廚房助理 ▶ 沒問題。

5 minutes later…

5分鐘後……

CF ▶ Now place the casserole in the oven for 30 minutes. <u>Sometimes it takes less than 30 minutes before the fish gets tender.</u>

25 minutes later⋯

CC ▶ Chef, I think the fish is done.

CF ▶ OK, transfer the fish to a heated platter and garnish it with the lemon slices and black olives.

CC ▶ Yes. Now we can serve it.

主廚 ▶ 現在把砂鍋放進烤箱烤30分鐘。有時候不用30分鐘魚就會變軟嫩了。

25分鐘後⋯⋯

廚房助理 ▶ 主廚，魚應該好了。

主廚 ▶ 好的，把魚放到加熱過的淺盤裡，然後用檸檬片和黑橄欖裝飾。

廚房助理 ▶ 是的，我們現在可以上菜了。

09 Unit

10 Unit

11 Unit

12 Unit

🍕 *Vocabulary* 字彙

1. **marinate** [`mærə͵net] **V** 動詞　把⋯⋯浸泡在滷汁中
   Marinate the veal with soy sauce, garlic, ginger, and rice wine for 2 hours.
   用醬油、大蒜、薑、米酒醃小牛肉兩小時。

2. **shallow** [`ʃælo] **adj** 形容詞　淺的
   The dish is too shallow to serve soup in.
   這盤子太淺無法盛湯。

3. **marinade** [ˌmærəˈned] **n** 名詞 （用酒、醋、油、香料等配成的）滷汁

Don't pour away the old marinade. It can be used next time.

不要把舊的滷汁丟掉。下次還可以用。

4. **tablespoon** [ˈtebl̩ˌspun] **n** 名詞 大湯匙，大調羹

Put a tablespoon of oil into the frying pan. We are frying beef.

倒一大匙的油進炒鍋。我們要炒牛肉。

5. **scale** [skel] **v** 動詞 去魚鱗

You have to make sure the fish are fully scaled

你務必要把魚鱗去乾淨。

6. **bone** [bon] **v** 動詞 剔去……的骨

Skin, bone and flake the fish.

去魚皮，魚骨後把魚切薄片。

7. **casserole** [ˈkæsəˌrol] **n** 名詞 砂鍋

Who made this casserole of beef?

這個砂鍋牛肉是誰做的？

8. **platter** [ˈplætɚ] **n** 名詞 大淺盤（通常為橢圓形）

Can you put these five kinds of cheese on a wooden platter?

你可以把這五種起司放在木製的大淺盤上嗎？

In Other Words 這樣說也能通

1. Are we still using it later?

我們待會還要用嗎?

✿ We will keep it for further use?

✿ We are using it later?

2. Now scale and bone the halibut.

現在把比目魚去鱗然後去骨。

✿ Now cut away the scale and bones of the halibut.

✿ Now scale and remove the bones of the halibut.

3. Now we will cook the pieces of fish in the casserole?

現在我們把魚片放在砂鍋裡煮嗎?

✿ Now we will use the casserole to cook the fish pieces?

✿ Now the fish pieces will be cooked in the casserole?

4. Sometimes it takes less than 30 minutes before the fish gets tender.

有時候不用30分鐘魚就會變軟嫩了。

✿ Sometimes the fish can get tender within 30 minutes.

✿ Sometimes it won't take more than 30 minutes to make the fish become tender.

Unit 11

Cooking- Main Courses
烹飪 – 主菜

11.2

Beef Stroganoff 俄式燉牛肉

 Dialogue 停不住對話

CC ▶ Commis Cook 廚師助理 **CF ▶ Chef** 主廚

CF ▶ Let's do beef stroganoff. Can you cut the beef into strips?

主廚 ▶ 我們現在來做俄式燉牛肉。你可以把牛肉切成條狀嗎？

CC ▶ Yes, I'm finished.

廚房助理 ▶ 好 的，我做完了。

CF ▶ Did you prepare the mushrooms, onions, and garlic?

主廚 ▶ 你有準備蘑菇、洋蔥、和大蒜嗎？

258

CC ▸ Yes, I've put them in a plate.

廚房助理 ▸ 有的，我把它們放在盤子上。

CF ▸ Good. <u>Use a frying pan</u> to cook them in butter now.

主廚 ▸ 很好。拿平底鍋用奶油煮。

09 Unit

CC ▸ Yes. Now cover it?

廚房助理 ▸ 好的，要蓋上蓋子嗎？

CF ▸ Yes, cover and simmer for about ten minutes. <u>Don't forget to stir it occasionally.</u>

主廚 ▸ 是，蓋上蓋子用小火慢燉大約10分鐘。不要忘記偶爾攪拌一下。

10 Unit

After ten minutes⋯

10分鐘後⋯⋯

11 Unit

CC ▸ I think the vegetables are pretty much done.

廚房助理 ▸ 我想蔬菜應該煮好了。

CF ▸ Remove them from the frying pan.

主廚 ▸ 把它們從平底鍋拿出來。

12 Unit

CC ▸ OK. Should I cook the beef now?

廚房助理 ▸ 好的。現在要煮牛肉了嗎？

CF ▸ You're right. Cook it over the medium heat for about ten minutes.

主廚 ▸ 答對了。用中火煮大約10分鐘。

After ten minutes⋯

10分鐘後⋯⋯

CC ▸ The ten minutes are up.

廚房助理 ▸ 十分鐘到了。

CF ▶ Add the water, bouillon, salt, and pepper, and heat it to a boil.

主廚 ▶ 加水、牛肉清湯、鹽、胡椒。然後加熱到沸騰。

CC ▶ Yes. Now it's boiling.

廚房助理 ▶ 好的。現在滾了。

CF ▶ OK, you can reduce the heat, and cover and simmer the beef.

主廚 ▶ 好的，現在把火關小，蓋上蓋子，然後小火慢燉牛肉。

CC ▶ For how long?

廚房助理 ▶ 煮多久呢？

CF ▶ <u>I will simmer for 15 minutes and then the beef can be nice and tender.</u>

主廚 ▶ 我會燉15分鐘，然後牛肉應該就會很軟嫩了。

After 15 minutes…

15分鐘後……

CC ▶ The beef is done.

廚房助理 ▶ 牛肉好了。

CF ▶ Please add the vegetable mixture of mushrooms, onions, and garlic in.

主廚 ▶ 請把蘑菇、洋蔥、和大蒜加進去。

CC ▶ I will heat it to a boil?

廚房助理 ▶ 加熱到沸騰嗎？

CF ▶ Yes, please and reduce the heat once it's boiling.

主廚 ▶ 是的。煮開後就把火關小。

CC ▸ OK, done.

主廚助理 ▸ 好 的， 做好了。

CF ▸ Stir in the sour cream and mustard to add flavor.

主廚 ▸ 把酸奶油和芥末醬攪拌進去增加風味。

CC ▸ Yes. How should I garnish the beef stroganoff?

廚房助理 ▸ 好 的。 我要怎麼裝飾這道俄式燉牛肉。

CF ▸ You can use parsley.

主廚 ▸ 你可以用荷蘭芹。

CC ▸ Got it.

廚房助理 ▸ 了解。

CF ▸ We serve the beef stroganoff with the choice of noodles or rice.

主廚 ▸ 我們用米飯和麵條搭配一起上這道菜。

CC ▸ OK, I will cook the noodles and rice now.

廚房助理 ▸ 好 的。 我現在煮飯和麵條。

Vocabulary 字彙

1. **stroganoff** [ˋstrɔgəˌnɔf]　adj 形容詞　俄式烹調的
The specials we are making today are beef stroganoff, chicken curry and lamb chops with mint sauce
我們今天要做的特色菜是俄式燉牛肉、咖哩雞、和薄荷醬羊排。

2. **mushroom** [ˋmʌʃrʊm] **n** 名詞 蘑菇
Do you still remember how to make mushroom omelets?
你還記得怎麼做蘑菇煎蛋餅嗎？

3. **garlic** [ˋgɑrlɪk] **n** 名詞 大蒜、蒜頭
Add ample garlic and a little sherry if you want to cook pieces of succulent chicken.
如果你要煮美味多汁的雞肉，多加點大蒜和少許雪莉酒。

4. **pan** [pæn] **n** 名詞 平底鍋
Put the onions in the pan and cook until lightly browned.
把洋蔥放到平底鍋中炒至略呈棕色。

5. **bouillon** [ˋbujɑn] **n** 名詞 （牛肉等的）清湯
Add some chicken bouillon when you fry the noodles.
炒麵時加入一些雞高湯。

6. **mixture** [ˋmɪkstʃɚ] **n** 名詞 混合物、混合料
Now you just alternate layers of that mixture and cheese.
現在你只需要把起司和拌料一層層交替放好。

7. **sour** [ˋsaʊr] **adj** 形容詞 酸的，酸味的
We will serve this spaghetti with marinara sauce and sour cream.
這道義大利麵會搭配義大利番茄醬和酸奶油。

8. **mustard** [ˋmʌstɚd] **n** 名詞 芥末
This meat can be seasoned with salt and mustard.
這個肉可以用鹽巴和芥末調味。

In Other Words 這樣說也能通

1. Use a frying pan to cook them in butter now.

拿平底鍋用奶油煮。

✨ Now you can cook them in butter with a frying pan.

✨ Cook them with butter in a frying pan.

2. Don't forget to stir it occasionally.

不要忘記偶爾攪拌一下。

✨ Remember to stir it occasionally.

✨ Don't forget to stir it from time to time.

3. I will simmer for 15 minutes and then the beef can be nice and tender.

我會燉15分鐘，然後牛肉應該就會很軟嫩了。

✨ The beef should be nice and tender after simmering for 15 minutes.

✨ I will simmer for 15 minutes to make the beef nice and tender.

4. We serve the beef stroganoff with the choice of noodles or rice.

我們用米飯和麵條搭配一起上這道菜。

✨ The beef stroganoff can go with either noodles or rice.

✨ The guests can choose to have the beef stroganoff with noodles or rice.

Unit 11

Cooking- Main Courses
烹飪 － 主菜

11.3 ## Chicken with Plum and Honey
梅子蜂蜜雞

Dialogue 停不住對話

CC ▶ Commis Cook 廚師助理 **CF** ▶ Chef 主廚

CF ▶ Today we will use this large jointed roasting chicken to make this new dish- chicken with plum and honey.

主廚▶今天我們會用這支帶骨烤雞來做這道新菜：梅子蜂蜜雞。

CC ▶ Woo, it sounds very delicious!

廚房助理 ▶ 哇，聽起來好美味。

CF ▶ Yes, it is. Please cut the roasting chicken into pieces first.

主廚▶是的，很美味。你可以先把這隻烤雞切塊。

CC ▶ No problem. And then?

廚房助理 ▶ 沒問題，然後呢？

CF ▶ Put the pieces of chicken into a large saucepan, and then add salt and pepper to taste along with the saffron, cinnamon stick, onion, and butter.

主廚 ▶ 把雞塊放入長柄煮鍋中，然後加適量鹽巴和胡椒、番紅花、肉桂條、洋蔥、和奶油。

CC ▶ I'm finished. <u>I think I will now pour in water to cover the chicken completely and bring it to a boil.</u>

廚房助理 ▶ 我做好了。我想我現在倒入水把雞肉完全淹蓋然後煮滾。

CF ▶ You're right. Once it's boiling, cover the pan and lower the heat and simmer it for around one hour.

主廚 ▶ 對。水滾之後就蓋上蓋子，然後把火關小，文火煮一小時。

One hour later…

1小時後……

CC ▶ It has been one hour, chef.

廚房助理 ▶ 主廚，已經一小時了。

CF ▶ Can you check if the chicken is tender now?

主廚 ▶ 你可以看一下雞肉軟了嗎？

CC ▶ Yes, it is.

廚房助理 ▶ 是的，軟嫩的。

CF ▶ Good. Then pick up the chicken pieces and put them on a plate.

主廚 ▶ 很好。然後挑出雞肉並放在盤子上。

CC ▶ OK. I think now I have to add the plums in the pan.

廚房助理 ▶ 好 的。 現在我要加梅子進去鍋裡。

CF ▶ Wait! You should remove the cinnamon stick first.

主廚 ▶ 等一下，你要先把肉桂條拿出來。

CC ▶ Oh, I see.

廚房助理 ▶ 喔， 知 道了。

CF ▶ Now you can add the plums, powdered cinnamon, and honey in, and cook gently for 15 minutes.

主廚 ▶ 你現在可以放入梅子、肉桂粉、蜂蜜進去，小火熬煮15分鐘。

CC ▶ Should I cover the pan or not?

廚房助理 ▶ 鍋 子 要 蓋上蓋子嗎？

CF ▶ No, simmer the ingredients uncovered.

主廚 ▶ 不用，小火燉煮這些食材，不用蓋蓋子。

CC ▶ And stir it occasionally?

廚房助理 ▶ 偶 爾 要 攪拌嗎？

CF ▶ Yes, you bet! Continue simmering until the sauce is as thick as syrupy.

主廚 ▶ 是 的，你 說 對了。繼續小火燉煮直到醬料和蜜糖一樣濃稠。

15 minutes later···

15 分鐘後……

CC ▶ The sauce is done.

廚房助理 ▶ 醬汁煮好了。

CF ▸ Put the chicken pieces into the pan, and continue cooking for another 10 minutes to reheat the chicken.

主廚 ▸ 把雞塊放回鍋中，繼續煮10分鐘重新加熱雞塊。

10 minutes later…

10分鐘後……

CC ▸ Time is up. Should I place the chicken on a heated platter?

廚房助理 ▸ 時間到。我要把雞塊放到預先加熱的淺盤裡嗎？

CF ▸ Yes, please. Pour the sauce and plums over the chicken.

主廚 ▸ 是的。把醬汁和梅子淋在雞肉上。

CC ▸ Should I garnish it?

廚房助理 ▸ 要裝飾嗎？

CF ▸ I've prepared some browned almonds and toasted sesame seeds. You can use them for garnish.

主廚 ▸ 我有準備一些褐色杏仁和烤芝麻。你可以用它們來裝飾。.

Vocabulary 字彙

1. **roast** [ˋrost]　Ⅴ 動詞　燒烤
You have to stuff the turkey before roasting it.
你要先把料填入火雞肚裡，然後再烤。

2. **plum** [plʌm]　ⓝ 名詞　洋李；梅子
Can you teach me how to make plum preserves?
你可以教我做梅子蜜餞嗎？

3. **cinnamon** [ˋsɪnəmən] 🄝 名詞　肉桂
I have to say cinnamon is an excellent flavor enhancer.
我必須說肉桂是絕佳的提味香料。

4. **thick** [θɪk]　adj 形容詞　濃的、黏稠的
Whip the cream until thick, please.
請把奶油打到黏稠。

5. **syrupy** [sɪrˋəpɪ]　adj 形容詞　似蜜糖的
Can you cook the marinade in a small saucepan over low heat until it gets syrupy?
你可以用小平底鍋小火煮醃料直到它變的濃稠嗎？

6. **heated** [ˋhitɪd]　adj 形容詞　熱的
Bake the biscuits in a pre-heated oven.
把餅乾放入預熱的烤箱中烤。

7. **almond** [ˋɑmənd]　🄝 名詞　杏仁，杏核
Would you please mix the milk, yoghurt, eggs, almond powder and sugar in the bowl?
請把牛奶、優格、蛋、杏仁粉、和糖在碗裡混合攪拌。

8. **sesame** [ˋsɛsəmɪ]　🄝 名詞　芝麻
Have you put some sesame crackers in the oven to bake?
你有把那幾片脆餅放進烤箱裡烤了嗎？

In Other Words 這樣說也能通

1. I think I will now pour in water to cover the chicken completely and bring it to a boil.
   我想我現在倒入水把雞肉完全淹蓋然後煮滾。
   - ✦ I think I will now pour in enough water to completely cover the chicken and bring it to a boil.
   - ✦ I think I will fully cover the chicken with water and bring it to a boil.

2. Should I cover the pan or not?
   鍋子要蓋上蓋子嗎?
   - ✦ Should the pan be covered or not?
   - ✦ I wonder if I have to cover the pan?

3. Simmer the ingredients uncovered.
   小火燉煮這些食材,不用蓋蓋子。
   - ✦ Simmer the ingredients without covering the pan.
   - ✦ Keep the pan open and simmer the ingredients.

4. Continue simmering until the sauce is as thick as syrupy.
   繼續小火燉煮直到醬料和蜜糖一樣濃稠。
   - ✦ Keep simmering till the sauce is as thick as syrupy.
   - ✦ Keep simmer the sauce until it becomes thick like syrupy.

Unit 11

Cooking- Main Courses
烹飪 － 主菜

11.4 Eggplant Omelet 茄子煎蛋捲

 Dialogue 停不住對話

CC ▶ Commis Cook 廚師助理　**CF** ▶ Chef 主廚

CF ▶ Now we are making eggplant omelet. Can you prepare the eggplants first?

主廚 ▶ 現在我們要做茄子煎蛋捲。你可以先準備茄子嗎？

CC ▶ Yes, how many eggplants do we need?

廚房助理 ▶ 好的。我們需要幾個茄子？

CF ▶ Three, please. Peel and cube them first.

主廚 ▶ 三個。先把它們去皮後切丁。

CC ▸ OK.

廚房助理 ▸ 好的。

CF ▸ Sprinkle the cubes with salt, and set them aside for half an hour. Meanwhile let's prepare onions and garlic.

主廚 ▸ 將茄子丁撒上鹽巴後，在一旁放置半小時。 同時我們來準備洋蔥和大蒜。

09
Unit

CC ▸ Yes, I will crush 3 cloves of garlic. How about onions?

廚房助理 ▸ 好 的。 我會壓碎三瓣大蒜。洋蔥呢？

10
Unit

CF ▸ Chop 2 medium sized onions finely, please.

主廚 ▸ 請把兩個中等大小的洋蔥切碎。

CC ▸ No problem.

廚房助理 ▸ 沒問題。

11
Unit

CF ▸ I think the salted eggplants are done. <u>Can you rinse them, and dry them with paper towels?</u>

主廚 ▸ 我想茄子應該醃好了。你可以用水清洗它們然後用紙巾擦乾嗎？

12
Unit

CC ▸ OK, done.

廚房助理 ▸ 好 的， 做好了。

CF ▸ Now I will show you how to cook the eggplant omelet. First, melt the butter in a large frying pan. Then add the onions and garlic and fry. Stir until the onions and garlic are soft. OK, now can you put the eggplant cubes in?

主廚 ▸ 現在我示範給你看如何做茄子煎蛋捲。首先，將奶油放進大煎鍋加熱融化。然後加入洋蔥和大蒜拌炒直到洋蔥和大蒜變軟。現在你可以把茄子丁加進去嗎？

CC ▶ Yes, I will cook them until tender.

廚房助理 ▶ 好的，我把茄子炒軟。

CF ▶ Next, pour in the eggs, and use a little bit of salt and pepper to season the ingredients.

主廚 ▶ 接下來把蛋倒進去，用一點鹽和胡椒把食材調味。

CC ▶ Sure, I will stir to mix the ingredients.

廚房助理 ▶ 好的。我把所有食材混和攪拌。

CF ▶ Now turn down the heat. Cover the frying pan.

主廚 ▶ 現在把爐火調小，蓋上煎鍋的蓋子。

CC ▶ How long should I cook the omelet?

廚房助理 ▶ 蛋捲要煮多久？

CF ▶ About 15 minutes, or until the bottom of the omelet is slightly set. I will preheat the grill now.

主廚 ▶ 大約15分鐘，或是煮到煎蛋捲的底部變硬。我現在先預熱烤架。

10 minutes later⋯

10分鐘後⋯⋯

CF ▶ Can you now place the frying pan beneath the grill?

主廚 ▶ 你可以現在把煎鍋放在烤架下烤嗎？

CC ▶ Yes, then what's next?

廚房助理 ▶ 好的，然後呢？

CF ▶ Grill the omelet until the top of it is cooked and lightly brown.

主廚 ▶ 烤到蛋捲表面熟了變成淺褐色。

CC ▶ No problem.

廚房助理 ▶ 沒問題。

Vocabulary 字彙

1. **eggplant** [`ɛg͵plænt] **n** 名詞　茄子
Our vegetarian pizza uses the tomato, eggplant, and mushrooms as the topping.
我們的素食披薩會鋪上一層番茄、茄子、和蘑菇。

2. **omelet** [`ɑmlɪt] **n** 名詞　煎蛋餅，煎蛋捲
I can easily whip up an omelet.
我可以很快地做好一份煎蛋捲。

3. **cube** [kjub] **v** 動詞　將……切成小方塊；將……切丁
Now remove the seeds and stones and cube the flesh.
現在把籽和果核去掉，然後把果肉切丁。

4. **crush** [krʌʃ] **v** 動詞　壓碎，壓壞；碾碎；榨
Do you want me to crush some orange juice?
你要我榨一些柳丁汁嗎？

5. **chop** [tʃɑp] **v** 動詞　切細，剁碎
Will you chop three tomatoes and one onion for me?
你可以幫我把三個番茄和一個洋蔥剁碎嗎？

6. **rinse** [rɪns] **v** 動詞　沖洗
Rinse the vegetables under cold running water for 15 minutes.
用涼的自來水清洗這些蔬菜15分鐘。

7. **melt** [mɛlt] **v** 動詞　使融化；融化
Please heat and melt butter in a large microwave-proof dish.
請用微波爐適用的大盤子加熱融化奶油。

8.**pepper** [`pɛpɚ]　**n** 名詞　胡椒粉；辣椒粉；香辛調味品
Roll the meat in finely ground black pepper to season it.
把肉在細磨的黑胡椒粉裡滾一下來調味。

In Other Words 這樣說也能通

1. Peel and cube them first.

先把它們去皮後切丁。

⭐ Peel and dice them first.
⭐ Remove the skin and cut them into cubes first.

2. Can you rinse them, and dry them with paper towels?

你可以用水清洗它們然後用紙巾擦乾嗎？

⭐ Can you use water to clean them and dry them with paper towels?
⭐ Can you wash them and then use paper towels to dry them?

3. Use a little bit of salt and pepper to season the ingredients.

用一點鹽和胡椒把食材調味。

⭐ Season the ingredients with a little bit salt and pepper.
⭐ Use a little salt and pepper to add flavor of the ingredients.

4. Now turn down the heat.

現在把爐火調小

⭐ Now turn down the heat to low.
⭐ Now low down the heat.

09
Unit

10
Unit

11
Unit

12
Unit

Unit 12

Baking-Desserts
烘焙 — 甜點

12.1 Black Forest Cake 黑森林蛋糕

 Dialogue 停不住對話 45

CC ▶ Commis Cook 廚師助理　　**CF ▶ Chef** 主廚

CF ▶ Have you greased and floured the two cake pans?

主廚▶你有在兩個蛋糕烤盤上抹奶油和灑麵粉了嗎?

CC ▶ Yes, I have.

廚房助理 ▶ 有。

CF ▶ Good. I will now preheat the oven to 400 degrees. Can you put the sugar, salt, water, flour, cocoa, baking soda, eggs, and vanilla in the mixer?

主廚▶很好。 我現在會把烤箱預熱到400度。 你可以把糖、鹽、水、麵粉、可可粉、泡打粉、蛋、和香草精放進攪拌機裡嗎?

276

CC ▸ No problem. Should we mix the ingredients at low, medium, or high speed?

廚房助理 ▸ 沒 問 題。我們要用低速，中速，還是高速攪拌材料？

CF ▸ <u>Mix them at low speed first, for thirty seconds, and then set it to high speed, for two minutes.</u>

主廚 ▸ 用低速攪拌30秒，然後轉到高速攪拌2分鐘。

CC ▸ Time's up. Should I pour the ingredients into the baking pans?

廚房助理 ▸ 時 間 到 了。要把攪拌好的材料倒進烤盤裡嗎？

CF ▸ Yes, and then put the two pans into the oven.

主廚 ▸ 是的。然後把這兩個烤盤放進烤箱。

CC ▸ For how long?

廚房助理 ▸ 請 問 要 烤 多久？

CF ▸ Approximately thirty minutes.

主廚 ▸ 大約30分鐘。

CC ▸ What can I do in the meantime?

廚房助理 ▸ 在 烤 蛋 糕 時我可以做什麼？

CF ▸ <u>Have you prepared the cherry filling?</u>

主廚 ▸ 你櫻桃餡做好了嗎？

CC ▸ Not yet.

廚房助理 ▸ 還沒。

CF ▸ Then you can make the filling now.

主廚 ▸ 那你現在可以做。

After 30 minutes…

CC ▶ The cakes are ready.

CF ▶ <u>Cool down the cakes on wire racks.</u>

CC ▶ OK.

After the cakes have cooled down…

CF ▶ I think the cakes are cool now. Now you can ice the cake with whipping cream, cherry filling, and sugar frosting.

CC ▶ No problem. What do we use to garnish the cakes?

CF ▶ I would like to use chocolate chips and fresh cherries.

CC ▶ OK, done. <u>Should I cut the two cakes into several portions</u>?

CF ▶ Cut each cake into eight pieces.

CC ▶ OK, I will set them aside?

30 分鐘後……

廚房助理 ▶ 蛋糕烤好了。

主廚 ▶ 把蛋糕放到金屬架上冷卻。

廚房助理 ▶ 好的。

蛋糕冷卻之後……

主廚 ▶ 我想蛋糕已冷卻了。你可以把鮮奶油、櫻桃餡、和糖霜抹上去了。

廚房助理 ▶ 沒問題。我們要用什麼裝飾蛋糕？

主廚 ▶ 我想用巧克力碎片和新鮮櫻桃做裝飾。

廚房助理 ▶ 好的，完成了。要不要把這兩個蛋糕切成幾等分？

主廚 ▶ 各切成 8 片。

廚房助理 ▶ 好的。先放置在一邊嗎？

CF ▶ No, we have to refrigerate the cakes.

主廚 ▶ 不，這些蛋糕要冰。

CC ▶ I see.

廚房助理 ▶ 了解。

 Vocabulary 字彙

1. **grease** [gris] **Ⅴ** 動詞　塗油脂於
Grease two baking sheets and heat the oven to 400 degrees.
把這兩個烤板抹些油，然後把烤箱加熱到400度。

2. **flour** [flaʊr] **Ⅴ** 動詞　撒粉於
Flour the pan, and put in the pie crusts.
把烤盤撒上麵粉，放入麵餅皮。

3. **mixer** [`mɪksɚ] **ⁿ** 名詞　攪拌器
This kind of mixer produces silky and even-textured batters.
這種攪拌器能攪拌出柔滑、質地均勻的麵糊。

4. **filling** [`fɪlɪŋ] **ⁿ** 名詞　（糕點的）餡料
Spread some of the filling over each pancake.
在每個煎餅上塗抹一些餡料。

5. **whipping** cream [ˈhwɪpɪŋ krim] **ⁿ** 名詞　鮮奶油
Can you first beat whipping cream until thick?
你可以先把鮮奶油打起備用嗎？

6.frosting [ˈfrɒstɪŋ] **n** 名詞　糖霜
I will prepare the frosting while baking the cake.
我會在蛋糕烘焙時準備糖霜。

7.portions [ˈporʃən] **n** 名詞　（食物等的）一份，一客
Can you divide the chicken soup into ten portions?
你可以把雞湯分成十等份嗎？

8.refrigerate [rɪˈfrɪdʒəˌret] **v** 動詞　（使）冷卻；冷藏；冷凍
Cover the meat with plastic film and refrigerate for 6 hours.
把肉覆上保鮮膜，冷藏六小時。

In Other Words 這樣說也能通

1. Mix them at low speed first, for thirty seconds, and then set it to high speed, for two minutes.
   用低速攪拌30秒，然後轉到高速攪拌2分鐘。
   ☆ At first, mix them at low speed and then do so at high speed for two minutes.
   ☆ Mix them first at low speed for thirty seconds and then high speed for two minutes.

2. Have you prepared the cherry filling?
   你櫻桃餡做好了嗎？
   ☆ Is the cherry filling done?
   ☆ Is the cherry filling ready?

3. Cool down the cakes on wire racks.
   把蛋糕放到金屬架上冷卻。
   ☆ Put the cakes on the wire racks to cool them down.
   ☆ Chill the cakes on wire racks.

4. Should I cut the two cakes into several portions?
   要不要把這兩個蛋糕切成幾等分？
   ☆ Should the two cakes be cut into several portions?
   ☆ Should I divide the two cakes into several portions?

09 Unit

10 Unit

11 Unit

12 Unit

Unit 12

Baking-Desserts
烘焙 － 甜點

| 12.2 | **Almond Crescent 弦月杏仁餅** |

 Dialogue 停不住對話 46

CC ▶ Commis Cook 廚師助理   **CF** ▶ Chef 主廚

CF ▶ We are making almond crescent now. I need 8 ounces of blanched almonds, 4 ounces of sugar, 6 tablespoons of rose water, 2 teaspoon of ground cinnamon, 2 beaten eggs, and 6 tablespoons of sesame seeds.

主廚 ▶ 我們現在要做半月型杏仁餅。我需要8盎司用水煮過去皮的杏仁，8盎司的糖，6大匙的玫瑰水，2小匙的肉桂粉，2個打好的蛋，和6大匙的芝麻籽。

CC ▶ No problem. All the ingredients are here.

廚房助理 ▶ 沒問題，所有的材料都在這裡。

CF ▸ Good. <u>Now put the almonds into a small saucepan, and then cover with water and simmer for 20 minutes.</u>

主廚 ▸ 很好，現在把杏仁放到小的長柄主鍋裡，加水覆蓋後用小火燉20分鐘。

20 minutes later…

20 分鐘後……

CC ▸ The almonds are done, I guess.

廚房助理 ▸ 我想杏仁應該煮好了。

CF ▸ OK, <u>now drain the almonds and use an electric blender to reduce them to a paste.</u>

主廚 ▸ 好的。現在把杏仁瀝乾，然後用電動攪拌機攪拌至糊狀。

CC ▸ Should I add a little bit of the cooking water in the blender?

廚房助理 ▸ 要加一點水到攪拌機裡嗎？

CF ▸ Yes, please. Can you also preheat the oven to 380 degrees?

主廚 ▸ 好的。你可以把烤箱預熱至380度嗎？

CC ▸ No problem.

廚房助理 ▸ 沒問題。

CF ▸ Now put the almond paste into a bowl, and give it to me.

主廚 ▸ 現在把杏仁糊倒進碗裡給我。

CC ▸ Here you are.

廚房助理 ▸ 給你。

CF ▸ I am adding sugar, cinnamon, and rose water into the bowl.

主廚 ▸ 我現在要加糖、肉桂、和玫瑰水到碗裡。

CC ▸ Yes, I will have to work the mixture into the firm dough?

廚房助理 ▸ 是，我把他們全部揉在一起？

09
Unit

10
Unit

11
Unit

12
Unit

CF ▶ Yes, and divide the mixture into walnut size balls.

主廚 ▶ 是的，然後把混和好的餡料分成一個個胡桃狀的小圓球。

CC ▶ Done. What's next?

廚房助理 ▶ 好了，然後呢？

CF ▶ Roll each ball between palms until they form a cigar shape.

主廚 ▶ 用掌心把每個小麵球搓成雪茄形狀。

CC ▶ How long should the cigar shape be?

廚房助理 ▶ 雪茄形狀的麵團要多長？

CF ▶ Make it two and half inches long. You also have to make it thicker in the middle than at the ends.

主廚 ▶ 2.5英吋長。麵團的中間要比兩端更厚。

CC ▶ No problem.

廚房助理 ▶ 沒問題。

CF ▶ When you are done, dip the "cigars" into the egg and then into the sesame seeds.

主廚 ▶ 做好後，把「雪茄形麵糰」沾上蛋汁，接著再沾芝麻籽。

CC ▶ OK, I will then shape them into crescents and arrange them on buttered baking tray?

廚房助理 ▶ 好的，然後我把他們捏成半月形狀，然後放在抹了奶油的烤盤上？

CF ▶ That's correct. Bake the almonds crescents in the oven for about 1 hour or until they become golden brown, and we are done!

主廚 ▶ 正確。把杏仁餅放入烤箱中烤大約一小時，或直到餅呈現金黃的棕色，然後我們就完成了。

Vocabulary 字彙

1.**blanch** [blæntʃ] **v** 動詞　用沸水燙（杏仁等）以便去皮
Have you blanched almonds by soaking off their skins in boiling water?.
你有把杏仁用沸水煮過去皮了嗎？

2.**drain** [dren] **v** 動詞　瀝乾
Drain the pasta first and then share it out between two plates.
把義大利麵瀝乾，然後平分到兩個盤子裡。

3.**blender** [`blɛndɚ] **n** 名詞　（做菜用）攪拌機
You can make some vegetable juice by chopping these vegetables and out them in the blender.
你可以把這些蔬菜剁碎然後放進攪拌機就可以做一些蔬菜汁。

4.**knead** [nid] **v** 動詞　揉成，捏製
Lightly knead the dough on a floured surface.
在撒上麵粉的檯面上輕輕搓揉這個麵團。

5.**walnut** [`wɔlnət] **n** 名詞　胡桃
The cake has a tasteful flavor consisting of Vanilla, Walnut & Honey.
這個蛋糕有香草、胡桃、和蜂蜜的可口味道。

6.**dip** [dɪp] **v** 動詞　浸；泡
Dip the fish pieces into the sauce so they are completely coated.
把魚片浸到醬汁裡使其完全被覆蓋。

7. **butter** [`bʌtɚ] Ⓥ 動詞　塗奶油於，以奶油調味
Butter the bread, please.
請把麵包塗上奶油。

8. **tray** [tre] Ⓝ 名詞　托盤；盤子
Place the defrosted meet rolls on a greased baking tray.
把解凍的肉捲放在抹了油的烤盤上。

 In Other Words 這樣說也能通

1. Now put the almonds into a small saucepan, and then cover with water and simmer for 20 minutes.
現在把杏仁放到小的長柄主鍋裡，加水覆蓋後用小火燉20分鐘。
✦ Cook the almonds in a small saucepan, and then cover them with water and simmer for 20 minutes.
✦ Cover the almonds with water in a small saucepan and simmer them for 20 minutes.

2. Now drain the almonds and use an electric blender to reduce them to a paste.
現在把杏仁瀝乾，然後用電動攪拌機攪拌至糊狀。
✦ Now drain the almonds first and then use an electric blender to make them into a paste.
✦ Now drain the almonds and reduce them to a paste by an electric blender.

3. You also have to make it thicker in the middle than at the ends.
麵團的中間要比兩端更厚。
  ⚝ The middle must be thicker than the ends.
  ⚝ You have to make sure the middle is thicker than the ends.

4. I will then shape them into crescents and arrange them on buttered baking tray?
然後我把它們捏成半月形狀，然後放在抹了奶油的烤盤上？
  ⚝ Should I make them into crescent shapes and arrange them on buttered baking tray?
  ⚝ Then I will shape them into crescents and put them on buttered baking tray?

Unit 12

Baking- Desserts
烘焙 – 甜點

 12.3 **Cheese Cake 起司蛋糕**

Dialogue 停不住對話

CC ▶ Commis Cook 廚師助理　**CF ▶ Chef** 主廚

CF ▶ <u>Can you mix the flour, sugar, and lemon rind in a small bowl?</u>

主廚 ▶ 你可以在一個小碗裡把麵粉、糖、和檸檬皮混和嗎？

CC ▶ Yes, and then?

廚房助理 ▶ 好的，然後呢？

CF ▶ Make a hole in the center, and place the egg yolk, butter, and vanilla essence in it.

主廚 ▶ 在麵團中間挖一個洞，然後把蛋黃、奶油、香草精放進去。

CC ▸ Done.

廚房助理 ▸ 做好了。

CF ▸ Look at me. I use my fingertips to mix the ingredients together to form a ball, and meanwhile make sure the dough comes away from the sides of the bowl.

主廚 ▸ 看我，我現在用指尖揉合材料直到形成一個球狀麵團，同時確認碗上沒有麵粉黏著。

CC ▸ What should we do with the dough, then?

廚房助理 ▸ 那揉好的麵糰接下來要怎麼做？

CF ▸ <u>Wrap the dough in aluminum foil and refrigerate for about 1 hour.</u>

主廚 ▸ 把麵團用鋁箔紙包起來，放到冰箱冰約一小時。

1 hour later···

1小時後……

CC ▸ It has been one hour.

廚房助理 ▸ 1小時了。

CF ▸ Good. Preheat the oven to 420 degrees now.

主廚 ▸ 很好。現在把烤箱遇熱到420度。

CC ▸ Yes, should I also lightly grease the bottom of a cake pan?

廚房助理 ▸ 好的。我要把烤盤底刷上一點奶油嗎？

CF ▸ Yes, please. Next, place half the pastry dough on a lightly floured board and roll it out.

主廚 ▸ 好的。接下來，將一半的派皮麵團放在沾了一點麵粉的板子上桿平。

CC ▸ And then place the dough on

廚房助理 ▸ 然後把麵

the bottom of the pan?

團放在烤盤上嗎？

CF ▸ Yes, remember to trim the edge.

主廚 ▸ 是的。記得沿著烤盤邊緣將多餘的麵團切斷。

CC ▸ No problem. Should I place the pan on the top, middle, or bottom shelf of the oven?

廚房助理 ▸ 沒問題。我應該把烤盤放在上層、中層、還是下層烤箱？

CF ▸ The middle shelf, please. Bake for about 15 minutes until the crust turns a pale gold. In the meantime, beat the cream cheese with a wooden spoon, and blend in the sugar, flour, orange and lemon rind along with the vanilla essence.

主廚 ▸ 請放中層。烘烤約15分鐘直到外皮呈現微微的金黃色。烤的時間用木鏟拍打奶油乳酪，然後將糖、麵粉、柳橙和檸檬皮、香草精拌入奶油乳酪中。

CC ▸ Should I also beat in the egg?

廚房助理 ▸ 要打蛋嗎？

CF ▸ Yes, but we have to separate the egg white and egg yolk.

主廚 ▸ 是的，但要把蛋白和蛋黃分開。

CC ▸ What should I do?

廚房助理 ▸ 要怎麼做？

CF ▸ Beat in the egg white first and then the egg yolks.

主廚 ▸ 先倒入一個蛋白攪拌，然後才是蛋黃。

CC ▸ Got you.

廚房助理 ▸ 知道了。

CF ▶ Now stir in the cream, and pour the mixture into the pale gold crust, and bake it in the oven for 15 minutes. When it's done, <u>make sure to cool the cheese cake for at least 2 hours before removing it from the cake pan.</u>

主廚 ▶ 現在加入奶油攪拌，把混合的餡料倒在金黃色的外皮上，然後放入烤箱烤15分鐘。完成後務必讓起司蛋糕冷卻至少兩小時，才能從烤盤上拿出來。

09 Unit

10 Unit

11 Unit

12 Unit

Vocabulary 字彙

1. **rind** [raɪnd]　**n** 名詞　（瓜、果等的）皮，外皮
Use a sharp knife to pare off the rind from the orange.
用一把鋒利的刀子把柳橙的外皮削去。

2. **dough** [do]　**n** 名詞　生麵糰
You have to add enough milk to form a soft dough.
你必須加足夠的牛奶才能做柔軟的麵團。

3. **wrap** [ræp]　**v** 動詞　包，裹
Cut the tuna into long strips and wrap it round the circumference of the bread.
把鮪魚切呈長條狀，然後包裹在麵包上。

4. **aluminum foil** [əˋlumɪnəm fɔɪl]　**ph** 片語　鋁箔紙
Can you wrap the fish with aluminum foil and then put it into the oven?
你可以把魚用鋁箔紙包起來然後放進烤箱嗎？

5.**pastry** [`pestrɪ] **n** 名詞　油酥（或其他配料的）麵糰；酥皮點心（如餡餅，水果派）

Roll out the pastry and cut into narrow and long strips.

把油酥麵糰　平然後切成細長條。

6.**trim** [trɪm] **v** 動詞　切除

You can use that knife to trim off the excess pastry.

你可以用那個刀子把多餘的餅皮切除。

7.**crust** [krʌst] **n** 名詞　麵包皮；派餅皮

Why is the crust of the bread burnt again?

麵包的外皮為什麼又烤焦了？

8.**beat** [bit] **v** 動詞　攪成糊狀

Blend the butter with the brown sugar and beat until light and creamy.

把奶油和紅糖混和在一起然後攪拌至滑軟細膩。

 In Other Words 這樣說也能通

1. Can you mix the flour, sugar, and lemon rind in a small bowl?

你可以在一個小碗裡把麵粉、糖、和檸檬皮混和嗎？

　✿ Can you add the flour, sugar, and lemon rind in the small bowl and mix them together?

　✿ Can you mix flour, sugar, and lemon rind all together in a small bowl?

2. Wrap the dough in aluminum foil and refrigerate for about 1 hour.

把麵團用鋁箔紙包起來，放到冰箱冰約一小時。

09
Unit

　☆ Use aluminum foil to wrap the dough and place it in the refrigerator for about 1 hour.

　☆ Wrap the dough with aluminum foil and cool it down in fridge for about 1 hour.

10
Unit

3. Beat the cream cheese with a wooden spoon, and blend in the sugar, flour, orange and lemon rind along with the vanilla essence.

用木鏟拍打奶油乳酪，然後將糖、麵粉、柳橙和檸檬皮、香草精拌入奶油乳酪中。

11
Unit

　☆ Use a wooden spoon to beat the cream cheese, and mix in the sugar, flour, orange and lemon rind as well as the vanilla essence.

　☆ Beat the cream cheese with a wooden spoon and blend it with the sugar, flour, orange, lemon rind, and vanilla essence.

12
Unit

4. Make sure to cool the cheese cake for at least 2 hours before removing it from the cake pan.

務必讓起司蛋糕冷卻至少兩小時，才能從烤盤上拿出來。

　☆ First you have to cool the cheese cake for at least 2 hours and then you can remove it from the cake pan.

　☆ You can't remove the cheese cake from the cake pan unless you have cooled the cake for at least 2 hours.

Unit 12

Baking-Desserts
烘焙 — 甜點

12.4

Strawberry Pie 草莓派

 Dialogue 停不住對話 🎧48

CC ▶ Commis Cook 廚師助理　**CF** ▶ Chef 主廚

CF ▶ Have you prebaked the pie crust?

主廚 ▶ 你有先烤好麵餅皮嗎？

CC ▶ Yes, I did, and now the crust has been cooled down to room temperature.

廚房助理 ▶ 有。現在餅皮已經冷卻至室溫了。

CF ▶ Good. Put the crust aside for now. Can you take out those strawberries in the fridge?

主廚 ▶ 很好。把餅皮放置在一旁。你現在可以把草莓從冰箱拿出來嗎？

CC ▶ OK, I will wash them first.

廚房助理 ▶ 好 的， 我 先把它們洗一洗。

CF ▶ And cut each strawberry into half.

主廚 ▶ 然後把每顆草莓 切成一半。

CC ▶ Done. What should I do next?

廚房助理 ▶ 好 了， 接 下來要做什麼？

CF ▶ Take out a saucepan, put in water, sugar, cornstarch, and strawberry gelatin. <u>Whisk the ingredients together well until they are thoroughly combined</u>, and then cook them over medium high heat

主廚 ▶ 拿一個長柄煮鍋 出來，加入水、糖、玉 米澱粉、草莓明膠，把 這些原料充分攪拌直到 它們完全混和。然後用 中大火煮。

CC ▶ Should I also constantly whisk the mixture while heating?

廚房助理 ▶ 在 加 熱 過 程中我也要不時攪拌這 些混合物嗎？

CF ▶ Yes, we do so to prevent clumping or scorching.

主廚 ▶ 是的，我們這樣 做來避免結塊或燒焦。

CC ▶ OK. Now the mixture has begun to come to gentle boil.

廚房助理 ▶ 好 的， 現 在混和物已經開始小滾 了。

CF ▶ You can now remove the pan from heat and allow the glaze to cool.

主廚 ▶ 你現在可以把鍋 子移開火爐讓糖漿冷 卻。

CC ▶ <u>What can I do to cool the glaze</u>

廚房助理 ▶ 我 要 怎 麼

quickly?

讓糖漿快速冷卻？

CF ▶ You can put some iced water in the sink and put the sauce pan into it. Remember to whisk occasionally as it cools.

主廚 ▶ 你可以在水槽內加點冷凍水，然後把鍋子放進去。記得在冷卻過程中要不時攪拌。

CC ▶ Good idea!

廚房助理 ▶ 好主意。

After 20 minutes…

20分鐘後……

CF ▶ Can you check if the glaze has become translucent in color?

主廚 ▶ 你可以看一下混和物顏色變成半透明了嗎？

CC ▶ Not quite.

廚房助理 ▶ 還沒。

CF ▶ OK, we will wait for another 10 minutes.

主廚 ▶ 好的，我們再等十分鐘。

10 minutes later…

10分鐘後……

CC ▶ Chef, the glaze now is translucent in color.

廚房助理 ▶ 主廚，糖漿現在顏色已經半透明了。

CF ▶ Good. Did it thicken a little more as well?

主廚 ▶ 很好。它也有變比較濃稠一點了嗎？

CC ▶ Yes, it did.

廚房助理 ▶ 有。

CF ▶ Bring the pie crust to me. I will add the sliced strawberries to the

主廚 ▶ 拿麵餅皮給我。我要把草莓切片加到麵

crust.

皮上。

CC ▶ Here you are.

廚房助理 ▶ 在這裡。

CF ▶ Thank you. Look, we are almost done! You just need to pour the glaze over the strawberries.

主廚 ▶ 謝謝。看，我們快做好了。你把糖漿淋到草莓上。

CC ▶ Sure.

廚房助理 ▶ 沒問題。

CF ▶ We have to chill the pie in the refrigerator for at least 2-3 hours before serving.

主廚 ▶ 我們必須把派放入冰箱冰兩到三小時才能端上桌。

Vocabulary 字彙

1. **cornstarch** [`kɔrnˌstɑrtʃ] **n** 名詞　玉米澱粉
   To make the moon shrimp cake, we need shrimp meat, cornstarch, pepper, salt, egg roll wrapper, chopped garlic, and chopped ginger.
   作月亮蝦餅我們需要蝦肉、玉米粉、胡椒、鹽、潤餅皮、蒜末、薑末。

2. **clump** [klʌmp] **v** 動詞　使凝結成塊
   Brown rice takes longer to cook but it doesn't clump easily.
   糙米要花比較多的時間煮，但它不容易結塊。

3. **scorch** [skɔrtʃ] **v** 動詞　把……燒焦，把……烤焦
The beef is likely to scorch if you leave it cooking too long.
這牛肉如果烤太久會焦的。

4. **glaze** [glez] **n** 名詞　（澆在食物上使呈光澤的）糖汁
Brush the glaze over the top and sides of the strawberry pie.
在草莓派的頂上和周圍都刷上糖漿。

5. **translucent** [træns`lusnt] **adj** 形容詞　半透明的
You have to cook the glaze until it becomes translucent in color.
你必須把糖漿煮到顏色變半透明。

6. **thicken** [`θɪkən] **v** 動詞　變濃
Beat the eggs and sugar until they start to thicken.
把蛋和糖攪打在一起直到它們變濃稠。

7. **sliced** [slaɪst] **adj** 形容詞　（食物）已切成薄片的
When the oil is hot, add the sliced onion and chopped garlic.
油熱了後，加入洋蔥切片和大蒜末。

8. **chill** [tʃɪl] **v** 動詞　使變冷
Chill the fruit salad before serving.
水果沙拉在端上桌前先冰鎮一下。

In Other Words 這樣說也能通

1. Whisk the ingredients together well until they are thoroughly combined

把這些原料充分攪拌直到它們完全混和。

⭐ Stir all the ingredients together fully until they are thoroughly combined.

⭐ Mix the ingredients together well until they are completely combined.

2. What can I do to cool the glaze quickly?

我要怎麼讓糖漿快速冷卻？

⭐ Can you tell me how to cool the glaze quickly?

⭐ Is there any way I can do to cool the glaze quickly?

3. Can you check if the glaze has become translucent in color?

你可以看一下混和物顏色變成半透明了嗎？

⭐ Can you go and see if the glaze has become translucent in color?

⭐ Can you check whether the glaze has become translucent in color or not?

4. Did it thicken a little more as well?

它也有變比較濃稠一點了嗎？

⭐ Did it also become thicker?

⭐ Has it become a bit thicker as well?

英語學習 —生活・文法・考用—

定價：NT$369元/K$115元
規格：320頁/17＊23cm/MP3

定價：NT$380元/HK$119元
規格：320頁/17＊23cm/MP3

定價：NT$349元/HK$109元
規格：352頁/17＊23cm

定價：NT$380元/HK$119元
規格：288頁/17＊23cm/MP3

定價：NT$329元/HK$103元
規格：352頁/17＊23cm

定價：NT$349元/HK$109元
規格：304頁/17＊23cm

定價：NT$380元/HK$119元
規格：352頁/17＊23cm

定價：NT$369元/HK$115元
規格：304頁/17＊23cm/MP3

定價：NT$380元/HK$119元
規格：304頁/17＊23cm/MP3

英語學習 —職場系列—

定價：NT$349元/HK$109元
規格：320頁/17＊23cm

定價：NT$360元/HK$113元
規格：328頁/17＊23cm

定價：NT$349元/HK$109元
規格：304頁/17＊23cm

定價：NT$360元/HK$113元
規格：320頁/17＊23cm

定價：NT$369元/HK$115元
規格：312頁/17＊23cm/MP3

定價：NT$369元/HK$115元
規格：320頁/17＊23cm

定價：NT$360元/HK$113元
規格：288頁/17＊23cm/MP3

定價：NT$329元/HK$103元
規格：304頁/17＊23cm

定價：NT$369元/HK$115元
規格：328頁/17＊23cm/MP3

Leader 030

一本搞定內外場餐飲英語 (附即答力 MP3)

作　　者	王郁琪	
發 行 人	周瑞德	
執行總監	齊心瑀	
企劃編輯	陳欣慧	
執行編輯	魏于婷	
校　　對	饒美君、陳韋佑	
封面構成	高鍾琪	

內頁構成	菩薩蠻數位文化有限公司
印　　製	大亞彩色印刷製版股份有限公司
初　　版	2015 年 11 月
定　　價	新台幣 380 元
出　　版	力得文化
電　　話	(02) 2351-2007
傳　　真	(02) 2351-0887
地　　址	100 台北市中正區福州街 1 號 10 樓之 2
E - m a i l	best.books.service@gmail.com
網　　址	www.bestbookstw.com

港澳地區總經銷	泛華發行代理有限公司
地　　址	香港新界將軍澳工業邨駿昌街 7 號 2 樓
電　　話	(852) 2798-2323
傳　　真	(852) 2796-5471

國家圖書館出版品預行編目資料

一本搞定內外場餐飲英語：全面提升你的英語即
答力 / 王郁琪著. -- 初版. -- 臺北市：力得文化,
2015.11
　面；　公分
ISBN 978-986-91914-9-4(平裝附光碟片)

　1.英語 2.餐飲業 3.會話

805.188　　　　　　　　　　　10402179